*To my best friend, my wife, and the
greatest blessing of my charmed life,
Clare.
You have made all the difference for
me, and for a troubled world.*
—*Austin Aslan*

*To baby deux, this story is for you.
As you embark on the grand adventure of life,
I hope it inspires you and reminds you of the power that
you have to change the world. Never forget that there is
always hope for the future, my little angel.*
—*Philippe Cousteau*

THE ENDANGEREDS

MELTING POINT

Also by Philippe Cousteau and Austin Aslan

The Endangereds

THE ENDANGEREDS

MELTING POINT

PHILIPPE COUSTEAU
AND AUSTIN ASLAN

HARPER

An Imprint of HarperCollinsPublishers

ISBN 978-0-06-289419-9

Typography by Corina Lupp
21 22 23 24 25   PC/LSCH   10 9 8 7 6 5 4 3 2 1

First Edition

PART ONE

CHAPTER ONE

WANGARI
(Phataginus tetradactyla)

Bahia Azul, Panama

Wangari, an African black-bellied pangolin, emerged from the jungle and spied the ruins.

"I have a visual," she reported through her headset.

The armor-plated mammal was not in her native woodland habitat. This was a Central American jungle, lush and humid, chock-full of exotic snack foods like New World leaf-cutter ants and target beetles. The ruins along the edge of the swamp were built by ancient Pana-manians and later retrofitted into a fortress by European settlers. Recently, the old structures had been made into a textile plant, where fabrics were dyed and sewn into clothes.

It was evening. The sun was low on the horizon, setting the wispy clouds ablaze over the nearby Caribbean Sea. The last of the factory workers were trickling past the crumbling wall at the forest edge toward their scattered bicycles and cars.

"I'll be all clear any minute."

"Copy that," Arief answered into Wan's earpiece. The orangutan's steady voice was always reassuring at the start of a tactical deployment. "We're standing by to extract you."

"Murdock, you're my eyes on this, right? Lead the way!"

"Uh, still hacking into the building schematics. I'll let you know what I find out. Meanwhile, proceed as planned, over."

Wan grumbled. But even if Murdock had detailed layouts at the ready, she would still need to trust her instincts tonight. Murdock was an arctic narwhal—a type of *whale*. His knack for the interiors of buildings was limited mostly to what he'd seen on television.

The factory workers finished shuffling out for the evening. Aside from the ever-present trilling of beetles and frogs, all was quiet.

"Time to make tracks," Wangari told herself.

She climbed the factory's outer stone wall. Finding plenty of grooves to grip with her powerful claws, she pulled herself up the centuries-old blocks with the ease of a lizard. Detecting a trip wire running the length of the wall top, she carefully sidestepped it. Wan crouched low and scanned the courtyard beyond.

The factory compounds rose three and four stories tall, matching the height of the jungle. The architecture was a mix of old and new, with windows and balconies on the upper floors. Vines clung to the rock faces. Cameras were affixed to all corners and motion-activated floodlights were perched along the rooftops. Guard dogs—a trio of rottweilers—roamed free, sniffing at the air and the grasses for a whiff of strangers. Human security officers were posted in places, relaxed but attentive.

At first glance, the guards could easily mistake Wan for a native coati or kinkajou or anteater, or something more domestic like a house cat. But over her armor of thick scales she wore a utility vest bulging with spy gadgetry. And her head was crowned with a formfitting night vision unit. If a sentry got a clean look at her, the operation could fall apart.

The dogs roamed out of sight into another courtyard around the corner. Wan tucked into a plated ball, rolled into the ferns, and uncurled, moving quickly toward the nearest building. Zigging and zagging across the open lawn, she dove to her belly when a man's voice rose nearby.

Her heartbeat picked up for a moment. If the guard spied her in the open, the mission would fail before it ever got going!

The human's voice turned against the breeze. *Now!* Wan thought. She lashed out her tongue. The tip wrapped around a woody branch of the vines clinging to the building's face. She half leaped, half reeled her way up onto the factory's exterior wall and began to scamper higher.

Her eyes targeted a curtain flapping through an open balcony window two stories above.

Something passed overhead. Wan gazed nervously toward the bulky movement, worried a large raptor might be on the hunt. But it was just a big seagull soaring by.

The dogs trotted back into view. Wan picked up the pace, latching her powerful digging claws into the old stone.

The canine sentries grew excited, sniffing the grasses far below. The first rottweiler loosened a bark as Wan reached the window and slipped inside, her utility harness catching momentarily against the sill.

I'm in, and not a moment too soon! she thought with a sigh of relief. *Now the fun begins.*

Wan had entered what looked to her like an expensive hotel suite, dimly lit only by the window. This wing of the factory must be where visiting corporate bigwigs, famous fashion designers and models, and high-dollar investors stayed over.

"Come out, come out, wherever you are," she summoned to the dark.

But her mission objective was probably deeper in the labyrinth ahead.

The pangolin abandoned the guest quarters, jumping up to open the door. The long corridor beyond was dark and empty. Fearing the presence of hidden cameras and infrared laser trip sensors, she pulled her night vision goggles down over her eyes and scanned the hallway again. Finding nothing out of the ordinary, she hurried farther into the palace interior.

She glanced into an open room and viewed a bank of computer monitors flicking through live images from throughout the compound. "Murdock, I'm at a security station," Wan whispered. A coffee mug vented steam along the countertop, but the chairs were vacant. "It's empty. But it won't be for long."

"Nice work. Find the master server and plug in the USB drive I gave you," the narwhal replied excitedly.

Someone would review tonight's recordings later once it became clear that a break-in had occurred. A bit of hard drive scrubbing was part of the plan—or images of a gymnast pangolin wearing a utility harness might end up all over the internet.

Wan rushed into the room and inserted the USB stick into a port. In addition to hacking the drives, they now had full backdoor access to the compound's security features. They could easily nab the schematics they were looking for too.

"I'm past the firewall with full system access!"

Murdock announced. "You can skedaddle, Wan. Stay alert for laser sensors. . . . I can't disable them without triggering a diagnostic sweep," he reminded her. "A warning alarm will go off."

"Copy that," Wangari answered.

She reached the grand staircase leading down to the lobby, and sure enough, her goggles revealed lasers crisscrossing every step in a sparkling green web. *How do I bypass that?* she thought, and then she saw a way. She sprang onto the railing and got down on her belly. Leaning her weight forward, nose-first, she bodyboarded down the curved banister, using her long tail as a brake.

"Stop!" Murdock barked over the comm.

Wan dug her tail into the railing and halted her descent. "What is it now?" she whispered.

"My video tracking indicates two bogies at the bottom of the staircase. Upper management, on account of their slick business suits."

"Thanks," she whispered. She took a deep breath, her heart still pounding in her chest, as she inched her way down the final few meters of the banister to avoid catching human eyes. When she reached the bottom, she dropped onto the cold hard tile and slunk around a large potted plant into another corridor.

"Nice job," Murdock said. "Now keep going about twenty yards and shoot left into the glass atrium between buildings. It's worth checking. There's a regular patrol in the area, so you only have about forty-five seconds before they come back around that corner."

Wan bounded down the hallway. She reached the atrium door, but it was locked. She could hear footsteps just around the corner. "A little help?"

"I'm working on it," replied Murdock.

"Well, work faster." Wan glanced over her shoulder and saw the leg of a security guard appear around the corner.

"Gotcha!" the narwhal trumpeted in her ear. The lock turned green, and Wan slipped through just in time.

From the looks of it, this area had once been outdoors, between buildings. But now a high, glass-paneled ceiling, held up by towering glass walls, enclosed the space. Like an enormous greenhouse, the air inside was hot and humid, reminding Wan of Arief's jungle hab back at the Ark.

Wan crept up behind one of numerous potted rain

forest ferns, scanning the enclosed courtyard. Natural light, now twilight-tinged and growing darker, filtered through the high glass ceiling. String lights draped between tall potted trees blinked on, illuminating the large, open area with an enchanting glow. Multiple security cameras were mounted along the atrium walls. "You reading this, Murdock?" Wan said.

"I got you covered. I'll put the security cameras on a ten-minute loop. No guards at the moment, so you're clear to move freely."

Block steps, in steep rows, ascended from the longer sides of a rectangular stone-tiled floor. Wan had wandered to the edge of a stone ballcourt, she realized, part of the original ruins built here by a culture from hundreds of years ago.

At the far end of the court was an animal enclosure, similar to the kind found in a zoo.

Now we're getting somewhere, she thought.

She spotted it: *Bradypus pygmaeus.*

A pygmy three-toed sloth.

It was small and all alone in the large enclosure, hugging a tree trunk about six feet off the ground. Sloths are nature's ultimate tree huggers, after all. With a stunted puppy-dog snout, its eyes were patterned with black fur like long streaks of eye mascara. Its shaggy hair was tinted green with algae—nothing unusual or unhealthy for its kind.

Wan stared across the distance with a growing half grin.

"Target acquired," she declared.

CHAPTER TWO

WANGARI
(Phataginus tetradactyla)

Wan rolled her neck and stepped forward onto the stone ballcourt floor.

Fewer than a couple hundred pygmy three-toed sloths existed in the wild. They lived mostly on Escudo Island, a small Caribbean atoll about ten miles off the coast from the factory. Pygmy three-toed sloths can swim, but that's not how this little fellow had gotten away from his home. He had been kidnapped by the owners of the textile plant.

The reasons why weren't clear to Wan or her team.

But when they'd learned that the critically endangered sloth had been imprisoned here, they knew they had to act—and fast. If the shaggy animal became too saturated by the smell of humans, the others of his kind might reject him, and with such a small population, losing even one individual from the gene pool could be catastrophic.

Wan felt her hind paw brush against something. She had forgotten caution, absently walking upright toward the target. She glanced down just in time to stop her foot from activating a trigger in the floor. A few feet to her left was a jungle rat, keeled over and motionless, its eyes wide open staring at her, a poison dart sticking out of its neck. *The floor's boobytrapped!* Wan gulped hard.

"Murdock, why didn't you warn me?"

"These traps aren't on the schematics. It's a rodent minefield! Activated after hours. These people aren't messing around. Be careful!"

"Great advice. Thanks," Wan joked.

Now that she knew to look for them, she detected other weight-sensitive plates disguised in the floor. She tip-clawed her way forward and arrived at the sloth's enclosure without depressing any.

Slowly, the sloth turned his head.

"Hey, buddy, I'm here to rescue you," Wan told the sloth.

"I'm going to sleep," the pigmy animal, a little smaller than Wan, eventually replied. "It's nighttime." The animal spoke in simple terms, and he understood Wan only in the way that all animals could understand each other.

"I have a better idea. Why don't you climb down?"

"Already?" The sloth yawned. "You just got here."

The pangolin rolled her eyes but took a deep breath. Wan and the other Endangereds were hyper intelligent. They could reason and plan. The sloth, on the other hand, was just an ordinary mammal. "Fine, I'll come to *you*."

The only door into the cage was along the side, with the wall of the stone ballcourt backing the enclosure. The door was padlocked. Wan patted her vest down, found her wire clippers, and moved toward the mesh, then thought better of it.

What if the fencing is electrified?

Wan inspected the structural supports framing the cage. She could see no obvious housing for a battery unit, no wrap-around insulators, no ground wiring. Wincing with anticipation, she tapped the mesh with the metal tip of her clippers, just in case.

No spark.

Wan shrugged. Using both of her front paws, she muscled the clippers shut and snapped through the first links.

A deafening alarm squelched to life, accompanied by flashing strobe lights.

"Deer droppings," Wan muttered. "I should have known better!"

"What is that?" managed the sloth after another yawn.

"No time to explain," Wan warned.

"There's always time," the sloth said.

Wan squirmed through the opening she had made by unlacing a few more links in the cables and then hustled up to the animal. "Hop on. Get a good grip."

The sloth obeyed. He was even relatively quick about it, transferring himself onto Wangari's back and latching on to the shoulder straps of Wan's harness with his hooklike claws.

Wan could feel a stampede of approaching human

footsteps in the hallways beyond the atrium doors. Determined not to be captured, or even seen, she galloped across the length of the ancient ballcourt, fleeing back the way she had come. There was no time to be careful or to avoid the booby traps. Poison darts shot from the walls. But Wan was too fast. The darts missed their marks, each whooshing behind her as she bounded forward.

Wan reached the patio that edged the interior courtyard just as two security guards barreled into the atrium from the north side. Wan skidded into hiding behind a giant slab of carved stone chiseled with ancient pictograms. Two more guards rushed into the atrium from the south. One of them flipped a switch on the wall, disengaging the poison dart system, and all four humans marched onto the ballcourt toward the sloth's enclosure.

At the same time, the steel double doors between the atrium and the hallway beyond began to swing shut. "We'll be trapped in here!" Wan cried. "Murdock, can you override?"

"Working on it . . . Best I can do is slow it down."

More security guards had entered from the southern corridor and were sweeping the atrium.

"Run for it!" yelled Murdock.

Wan broke her cover and bolted for the closing doors. She dove headfirst across the shiny tiles. The sloth cried out with delight.

Wangari made it! But the sloth lost his grip and tumbled off Wan's back. Wan flicked her tail and grabbed one of the sloth's arms and yanked him through. The doors slammed shut just as the sloth's hind legs were dragged to safety.

The animal's eyes were wide. "You're fast."

"We're not out of this yet," Wan promised.

"You can say that again," piped in Murdock. "Security guards are bearing down from both ends of the corridor. I'm shutting down the lights to buy you some time. There's an air conditioning shaft right above you. . . ."

"Copy that." With her night vision goggles activated, she glanced up at the AC panel and fidgeted blindly for a tool on her harness. The doors at the end of the corridor flew open, and two dogs rushed through. For one brief moment, Wan locked green-tinted eyes with the angry canines.

She unholstered her suction cup launcher, fired it, and whirled toward the ceiling. The dogs suddenly found themselves snapping at thin air.

With a quick thrust of her shoulder, the AC panel opened, and Wan and the sloth were safely inside. The dogs snarled and grunted, pacing. Their claws against the tile sounded like meat cleavers to Wan's ears.

"Orange leader, do you read?"

"Copy," Arief answered immediately. It was an enormous relief to hear the wise orangutan's voice. "What's your status?"

"Critically endangered," Wan quipped. "On the verge of extinction, as a matter of fact. Requesting emergency extraction."

"The main building's eastern courtyard has the most clearance. If you can make it there, we'll drop you a line, over."

"Copy that."

The sloth saddled up, and Wan was off at a gallop through the air-conditioning conduit. Within moments, however, they'd hit the end of the duct.

"Where to now?"

"You'll have to drop down into the main lobby below. Hurry," advised Murdock.

Wan opened the nearest grating and descended from her cup launcher like a spider.

As she and the sloth turned the next corner, three rottweilers burst through the lobby doors, all teeth and pink gums and clacking claws.

Wan instinctively pivoted through the nearest doorway. The light on the lock switched from green to red as Murdock remotely sealed the door.

Wangari exhaled a deep sigh of relief.

"Look. Isn't that a sloth?" noted the sloth, pointing a long claw up at the wall.

He was indicating an event invitation pinned to the office's bulletin board, featuring a picture of a three-toed sloth. Wan only caught the heading:

FASHION MASQUERADE BALL
CELEBRATE SCENIC TRAILS'S NEW LINE
OF CHILDREN'S OUTDOOR CLOTHING

FEATURING BRI-LEN AS EMCEE!

"I think that's *you*," Wan said. Underneath the sloth's picture was a caption reading:

HAVE YOUR PHOTO TAKEN HOLDING AN
EXTREMELY RARE AND IRRESISTIBLE PYGMY SLOTH.
PROCEEDS TO HELP CONSERVATION EFFORTS.

Wangari growled menacingly. "Conservation efforts my scaly butt." She tore the invitation from the board, folded it, and pocketed it for later inspection. "These animals need to be left alone on their island where they can try to thrive on their own terms."

"What was that? I didn't copy," chimed in Nukilik the polar bear over the airwaves.

Wan forgot that she had been transmitting. "Nothing. I'll fill you in later." She turned to the sloth. "Hop on. Those dogs will be back."

"That's not all. Security is swarming out from the atrium in your direction," reported Murdock. "Nearest extraction point is due west down the hallway, take your second left, get through the factory floor, then head down the eastern corridor to a window and you're home free."

"I'm following what you're seeing from my dashboard," said Nukilik. "We'll hover nearby until you reach the exit. We're airborne. ETA two minutes."

In the background of the transmission, Wan could hear the whirr of *Red Tail*, the team's tilt-rotor aircraft, which could fly like a plane but take off and land like a helicopter.

She made a break for the corridor, her progress and speed slowed by her live cargo.

Wan entered a warehouse filled with machines. A few sewing units were going, run by a woman wearing noise-canceling headphones. She watched a bank of spools feed fibers into one of several forty-foot-long looms. The threads were woven into patterned bolts of fabric. The clanking, grinding machinery was deafening.

"Any ideas?"

"Take exit number five," Murdock instructed.

Wan found the enormous sewing contraption marked with a black 5 and hurried through the door beside it.

The new hallway was as long as the previous one, ending in the distance at a closed window looking out upon the night.

A dog bark pierced the machine noises behind her.

Wan didn't glance back. She bounded toward the dead end on all fours.

She reached the closed window and sprang up on the narrow sill. The latch was loose, but the window was too heavy for Wan to lift on her own.

The dogs were half the distance to their goal and

licking their chops as they ran.

Wan plucked her glass cutter from her vest, gave it a hard look, and then simply used it to smash the windowpane.

"Wait! Wan! Don't—" Murdock's warning came too late.

A new alarm roared. Floodlights lit up the exterior grounds.

"See what I mean?" Murdock complained.

The dogs snarled victoriously, approaching their cornered prey.

"I'm out of time," Wan urged. She leaned forward toward the night but hesitated at the threshold. The ground below was rocky. Diving out the window wasn't an option, especially with a critically endangered hitchhiker strapped to her back.

And then a rope ladder dangled into view. Wangari smiled.

"We're in position," came Arief's welcome voice.

"Hang on tight," Wan told the sloth as a dog leaped for the pangolin, jaws wide open.

"I always do."

The rottweiler reached out the window and grasped at the air.

"Too slow!" Wan teased it, leaping for the ladder at the same moment. She clasped on to the lowest rung. She and the sloth were immediately yanked upward, spinning like a lopsided yo-yo at the end of a rocking string. The acceleration was intense as *Red Tail* rose and banked toward the sea, but both animals held fast.

"Too slow is right!" The tiny sloth cheered. He cried out with a wild thrill of pure delight, gulping back the salty wind while hollering, "Faster! Go faster!"

CHAPTER THREE

ARIEF
(Pongo abelii)

Isla Escudo de Veraguas, Panama

Red Tail touched down on a bit of high ground in a small clearing among the mangroves. Escudo Island was only a couple square miles is size, not much bigger than New York City's Central Park. It was ten miles offshore from the textile plant and was not supposed to have human inhabitants. On the books, the isle belonged to the pygmy sloths, but humans were known to come to the island to cut down trees and plant crops and fish the waters.

And so it went with the humans—all over the globe.

Time and again. Too little, too late. Arief knew the pattern well, from decades of painful experience and personal traumas.

An image of his mother and older brother getting brutally beaten by a band of armed men flashed in front of his eyes. He pushed the memory back.

Even when the humans tried to be responsible—and to their credit they sometimes did—they often fell short, or their efforts were undermined by other humans. Arief understood why local humans sometimes used the land the way they did, and it had everything to do with the fact that people didn't seem to like to share with other people. Humans needed to feed their families. Too often, many had no choice but to take what they could from the land just to survive, even when they understood the damage their actions would have on the environment over the long haul.

The tilt-rotor's propellers slowed to a halt, and the wildlife of the mangrove swamp resumed its chirping and buzzing and trilling. Arief opened the aircraft's main hatch with a push of a button and removed his headset. "We shouldn't linger here long," he told everyone on board. "It'll take us all night to reach the Arctic by morning."

The team's next objective was already lined up: find out the status of Nukilik's mother, and if she was indeed alive, reunite the two.

"Our search must begin after daybreak," the polar bear reminded them. "My mother will be most active then and easier to spot against the landscape while her shadow is long."

"I'm more worried about our refueling window!" Murdock insisted from his water tank at the rear of *Red Tail*'s cargo hold. "The filling station in Nova Scotia is only automated at night. Otherwise a human attendant will be snooping around, wanting to talk to our hairy pilot and verify our bank routing number."

"I'll be brief," Wangari promised, escorting the pygmy three-toed sloth down the ramp while holding his hand.

The pangolin turned to face her new friend when they reached the ground. "You know where you are? How to find home from here?"

Unhurriedly, the sloth turned his neck almost fully around like an owl to scan the jungle clearing. "I know this spot. I used to hang out with some buddies right over there." He slowly raised an arm and pointed a claw toward a forest wall where the branches blended in with the canopy of other trees.

A rather large bird flushed into the air from the dark hollows along the forest edge, as if the sloth had spooked it by pointing at it. With powerful wing flaps, it vanished into the dark.

"Do you mind if we keep tabs on you?" Wangari asked. But she wasn't really offering a choice. She had already produced a tiny tracking device and was moving to affix it onto the sloth's back, where it would remain hidden beneath his fur. "This'll help us monitor your progress after we leave. It'll pinch at first."

"That's fine . . . ow . . . with me," the sloth replied too late.

Wangari patted his new friend on the shoulder. "Be safe. Try to avoid the humans from now on. Hide as best you can when they come around."

"If you're ever in trouble," Arief said from the rampway, "we've made it our calling to protect any threatened or endangered animal or species that's in need. If you have a problem, if no one else can help . . . you can count on the Endangereds."

The tiny sloth gave Arief a slightly confused look but

offered him a grateful nod anyway as he slowly turned and disappeared into the jungle.

"All right, slowpokes!" Murdock insisted. "Round 'em up! Move 'em out!"

"Should I take the first shift at the helm? Or do you want it?" Nukilik asked Arief.

"You choose," he answered.

"Wait!" cried Murdock. "You can't let her decide. Don't you know better? Nukilik *always* choses wrong."

"Don't start with that!" Nukilik complained.

"It's true!" Murdock pressed on. "Weirdest thing: I've never seen her win a coin toss. We started tossing for chores a while back. It's getting to be eerie."

"No one can always get a coin flip wrong," Wan scolded. "It's statistically impossible."

"Try it," Murdock dared.

Wan took the bait. She scooped up a coin from the center console tray and flicked it in the air. "Call it, Nuk!"

"Heads," she said, sighing heavily.

The coin landed on tails.

Intrigued, Wan repeated the experiment four more times. Nukilik was dead wrong with each flip.

"All right, enough," Arief said. "I'm taking first shift, okay? Let's strap in already."

A moment later, Arief donned his headset and executed the preflight checklist. Nukilik was bent over the dash displays, double-checking the destination coordinates she had already quadruple-checked earlier. She plugged a few updated numbers into the autopilot.

"Buckle in, Wan," the great ape instructed. "Better take your seasickness meds, Murdock."

"I don't get seasick!" complained Murdock from his tank. "I get airsick. There's a difference."

"It all looks the same coming up," Nukilik pointed out.

The narwhal blubbered in offense, retreating toward the back of his tight saltwater quarters.

Wangari settled into her seat behind the orangutan and tapped him on the shoulder with something. "I found this in one of the offices downstairs," she explained. "Thought you might like a look."

Arief glanced back and took the piece of paper she was holding. It was made of thick card stock, decorated with fancy silver designs along the borders, and had a close-up mug shot of a pygmy three-toed sloth, possibly the same individual they had just rescued, though he couldn't be sure.

Arief took a moment to read through the fashion gala invitation. "This is a joke," he said, thrusting the note back at Wan. "Raising money? What they're doing is the opposite of conservation!"

"Those were my sentiments exactly," Wan told him.

"If we had more time, I would've liked to do more recon out here," Arief mentioned. "Clearly these humans are up to something. The fashion industry is a huge culprit when it comes to polluting the environment and causing climate change."

Murdock barked a chuckle from his tank. "We're fashion police now?"

"I'm really glad we were successful tonight." Arief allowed himself a rare smile. "Getting that poor animal safely home was the real victory. But it's a nice bonus, knowing we've rained on the parade of these corporate hyenas."

Red Tail, painted all black except for a distinctive red stripe slanting down the tilt-rotor's aft vertical stabilizers, lifted off like a helicopter and disappeared into the night sky.

CHAPTER FOUR

NUKILIK
(Ursus maritimus)

Baffin Bay, Greenland

"Arriving at your destination," the autopilot's monotone voice announced.

Nuk had dozed off some time ago, but now she shot up in her seat and put her paws around the aircraft's secondary controls.

Finally, I'm home! she thought with a thrill. The realization was accompanied by a nervous churning of her gut. *Mother . . .*

"Steady, gal. I got her," said Arief from the captain's chair beside her. The orangutan was wide awake. He was already gripping the primary controls with his hands, guiding *Red Tail* through a patch of turbulence.

Although the sun hadn't risen yet, the sky ahead wasn't dark anymore. The atmosphere contained a familiar pastel hue that Nukilik had missed since leaving the Great Realm. Down near the world's equator, where the Endangereds' HQ was located, the sun rose and set quickly, remaining high overhead for most of each day. It blazed against a washed-out sky. At the poles, however, the sun tended to linger low, sliding along the horizon for hours and hours. In the Arctic summertime, the sun never quite set. And in the dead of polar winter, it never actually rose but would hide shyly behind the mountains and glaciers for an hour or two before retreating fully back beneath the world.

During the present time of year, the Arctic sun wanted it both ways, rising and setting with great patience. The beautiful pastels of dawn persisted in the sky for hours. The soft pinks filled Nukilik with warm anticipation.

"You let me fall asleep," Nuk chided. "I told you not to."

"You needed the rest," Arief said. "Today's a big day."

"What about you?" Nukilik asked.

"I don't sleep well, anyway," the ape admitted. "It's okay, Nuk."

The polar bear stretched herself awake as much as possible while sitting in her cramped seat. She studied her copilot closely. She wasn't really familiar with Arief's sleeping habits. They kept to their own habitats during the nighttime at the Ark, the glass dome on the Galápagos Islands the Endangereds called home.

The original idea of the Ark was that it was supposed to be a place for threatened animals to remain wild until their native habitats were safe for them to return home. A lack of humans was an essential part of the Ark's purpose: no wild animal would become too accustomed to people. This clever design element made it far easier for the hyperintelligent Endangereds to come and go as they pleased.

"Rerouting," the autopilot proclaimed. *Red Tail* banked heavily to the left.

"Stop that." With a grunt, Arief took full control of the aircraft.

"Who voices these robotic guides?" Murdock wondered behind them, his head and long tusk poking above the water's surface of his tank. "'*Rerouting.*' Very patronizing. Like what they're really saying is 'You missed your turn, idiot.'"

"We haven't missed our turn," Arief pointed out. "Our destination is a pretty big area. No telling where exactly we'll find Nuk's mom. But this is where you last saw her, correct?"

No telling if we'll find her at all. That knot in Nuk's gut tightened another turn.

Nuk leaned forward in her seat for a better view out of the cockpit windows. The coast appeared as Arief gently circled the sky. "Yes," she said with confidence. She spotted the distinctive rocky formation that jutted out into the sea. It had taken her ages of searching the computers back at the Ark to find these coordinates. "This is definitely where I grew up."

That nervous energy in her stomach ballooned. Nuk wanted to blame the turbulence for upsetting her insides. But the sinking feeling had nothing to do with the flight. The last time Nukilik had been with her mother, they were swimming and exhausted, and became separated by a large human ship that passed by. Nuk never saw her mother again.

She grabbed for a bone to chew.

Arief must have read her thoughts. "She's down there," he assured her. "And remember: if we don't find her immediately, that doesn't necessarily mean the worst."

Nukilik gave her bone a turn and ground her jaws into it.

"Look at those waters!" Murdock beamed. "I can't wait to go for a swim."

"It's beautiful," Arief said.

"The Great Realm," declared Nukilik. "There's nothing prettier on the planet, especially when the green ribbons are flaring at night."

"Aurora borealis?" Arief asked. "I wish we could see that, but I hope we're not here long enough for night to fall."

Nuk spotted familiar islands away from Greenland's coast, noting that the ice sheet that seasonally connected them to the mainland was long gone. She spied only a few icebergs floating in the bay. And the glaciers that loomed over the valleys, with their tall, dramatic ice cliffs, were farther to the north than they should have been.

"It doesn't feel right," Nukilik said. She gestured out the window. "There should be more ice over the water this time of year. My ancestors used to reach those islands on foot, or with just a little swimming. I don't know how I know that, but the truth of it is in my bones."

"We carry the clocks of our mother's mother's mothers," Arief said. "It's hard for any animal to adjust what we see and feel these days to what we know should be true."

"And you've said the humans have done this?" Nuk asked.

"That's right," Murdock answered. "With all the greenhouse gases they've put into the air. The atmosphere traps more heat than it used to, which is why the ice is melting faster each spring and accumulating less during the winters."

Arief pushed in on the wheel, and *Red Tail* dove. The snow-covered landscape, patchy in places, grew large through the windshield. "Somebody wake up the pangolin," he suggested. "I'm going to switch to helicopter mode, and I don't want the jolt to surprise her."

Nuk reached back and gave Wan a nudge. "We're here."

Just then the sun breached the horizon, casting a warm yellow light across the landscape.

Wangari rubbed her eyes and sat up to look out the cockpit windows. "Look at all that snow!" she exclaimed with a shiver. She donned her goggles and cycled through an assortment of lenses before settling on sunglass filters.

The aircraft swooped and then hovered as the propellers transitioned from forward-facing to upward-facing. Arief descended to a hovering altitude low enough to give them a clear look at the ground but high enough not to bother wildlife.

With the sun peaking above the distant mountain line, the ground jumped out at them with more texture.

"There." Arief pointed to a rocky slope of tundra patched with snow, where polar bears were loosely gathered.

"It's a flock of Nukiliks!" joked Murdock. "Run for the hills!"

"A group of polar bears is called a sleuth, not a flock," Wangari said.

"Will wonders never cease?" said the narwhal.

"Is your mother likely to be among them?" Arief asked.

"I don't know," Nukilik answered. "If not, we can ask this sleuth if they know where she is."

"Good idea," Arief agreed. "I'll touch down by the water. Maybe let Murdock out to play while we're at it."

"Oh, thanks, Dad," Murdock griped.

"You must be excited," Wan told the narwhal. "You're back home too. Going to look up any relatives?"

"Meh." Murdock shrugged his vestigial shoulders. "This isn't my 'hood,'" he offered. "My pod's more likely to be chillin' on Greenland's east coast. But I'm still ready for a little time under the waves."

"You've earned a few splashes," Arief added. "Enjoy the cold water. But don't roam far."

"I promise not to migrate," said Murdock, "unless if I find an all-you-can-slurp shrimp buffet on the move. Then all bets are off."

"Ready? Set. Flush." Arief pulled a lever.

"Flush?" Murdock objected. "What do you take me for? Some kind of giant tur—"

The narwhal never finished his thought. *Red Tail*'s rear cargo hatch yawned open. The back wall of Murdock's tank rose. Water gushed out of the belly of the aircraft, showering the bay, and the two-ton occupant plopped out with it.

"Petunias!" Murdock cried as he plummeted into the sea with an enormous splash.

Red Tail sprang skyward, suddenly light and spry. Arief had to throttle down, cutting extra power to the blades.

Wangari winced. "Now that's what I call a belly flop."

Murdock surfaced after a few seconds, his tusk piercing the air first.

"Watch out, world!" he cried out joyfully. "Murdock's back in the north! And he's tusking for trouble!"

CHAPTER FIVE

ARIEF

(Pongo abelii)

Arief positioned the aircraft over the pebbly beach and then let the tilt-rotor's auto-landing function do the work. *Red Tail* set herself down beside the gentle surf.

"I'll keep an eye on things bayside." The narwhal came through loud and clear in Arief's ear. Murdock's headset was attached near his tympanic membrane and disguised to look like a barnacle. It had become a semi-permanent fixture on his head. "I forgot to wish Nukilik good luck. Tell her to break a leg for me. Never mind. Don't say that. No telling whose leg she'll break."

Arief hopped to the ground, his breath rising in a visible plume, the cold air stinging his nostrils. Wangari followed. Her breath lifted too. The field of snow upslope stretched off in all directions glistening white in the low-angle sunlight. It was surprisingly beautiful. Arief had never touched snow before and was surprised at what it felt like.

Nukilik came down the ramp, and Arief stepped politely aside. Nuk hit the beach and stood tall on her hind legs, eyes closed, reaching her snout toward the sky as the ocean breeze rustled the hairs of her belly and neck. She pawed the air and growled with delight. "It's good to be home."

Arief smiled for her benefit. He had not set foot on Sumatra since long before going hyper, and often wondered how it would feel to return. He imagined that his reaction might be similar.

But then awful memories came rushing back.

Mom and brother are netted and beaten, dragged into a cage on the bed of a truck. The infant Arief watches, helpless, from the treetops as Mom's arm go limp against the steel bars and as his older brother releases a final gasp of his own. . . .

A variety of seabirds and shore birds rose to flight then, soaring high along the bay's coast. Arief shook off the memory by focusing on their beautiful calls.

Nukilik turned to the ape, her dark eyes full of pride. "Isn't it lovely?" she asked.

The orangutan blinked. Actually, the Arctic wasn't really his scene. Where were the trees? He felt exposed here, not only to potential predators, but also to the elements. The wind was persistent and biting. He imagined that would soon grow tiresome. The sun, as low as it was, already felt intense. The snow was almost blinding. The sheer vastness of the distances between things unnerved him. But Arief was a wise old diplomat, and he understood where the polar bear's pride was coming from. "It is, Nukilik," he answered with a smile, adding, "but I'm glad I'm wearing a coat."

She looked inland, in the direction of the polar bears they had spotted from the air, saying, "I'm heading off. If you plan on tagging along, leave me some space, but try and keep up."

Nuk set out. Arief hastily fetched a pair of sunglasses from the supplies on board *Red Tail* and knuckled his way over the pebbled beach in pursuit of Nukilik.

"Sexy shades," Murdock commented into his earpiece, watching from somewhere off shore. "You look like a hairy Tom Cruise."

Arief ignored the comment.

"Oh, hey, you left the cockpit open," the narwhal continued.

Arief glanced at the aircraft but it was too late for him to turn back. Nukilik was covering so much ground that he feared he might lose track of her behind one of the hills. "Just keep an eye on it," he told Murdock.

Arief caught up to Wangari and both of them paused as they reached the snow. The orangutan ventured out a hand and scooped up a palmful. He couldn't hold back a nervous but amused laugh. It wasn't so cold, at first. Heavy and wet. He pressed it into his fist, packing it down. And suddenly it did feel cold. He threw the clump at Wangari, where it struck her plated shell and exploded. He laughed again.

"This means war," Wangari threatened. "Or you can make it up to me by giving me a ride."

Arief winked and hoisted the pangolin onto his shoulder. They set out over the snow, sticking to Nukilik's fresh tracks.

"How do you suppose this fact-finding mission is going to end?" Wan asked.

"I'm worried," Arief admitted, "but we need to let Nukilik see this through."

Of course, Arief knew there was a good chance they'd never find Nukilik's mother. What then? Would Nuk insist they keep looking? Would she remain behind to continue the search if Arief insisted it was time to load up and go? Or would Nuk play along and then demand later they return here again?

Or what if they did find evidence of the mother— evidence that she had . . . died? Arief had no way of predicting how Nuk would react to that news, but the very thought of it frightened him.

He picked up his pace in order to catch up with the determined polar bear.

CHAPTER SIX

MURDOCK
(Monodon monoceros)

Suddenly alone, Murdock's first instinct was to find a screen to tap on. He had a craving for a game of Minesweeper, but then he remembered that he was in the middle of the ocean.

No electronics! He sighed bubbles. *Gonna have to entertain myself out here, I guess.*

"Shall I peruse the local seafood aisle?" he asked himself.

Murdock's gut grumbled enthusiastically at the idea. "That sounds delectable," he decided. "Let's do it."

He took a big breath, ready to plunge deeper into the bay, when a large bird standing on the shore between him and *Red Tail* caught his attention.

What is that? he wondered. *I've been away from the wild for too long.*

The bird was mostly white with a few darker markings. Which put it in the same category as almost every bird evolved to survive in a snowy landscape. But it was noticeably large. In fact, because it was so big, Murdock realized that it was positioned closer to *Red Tail* than his eyes had first judged.

"A common eider?" he thought. "Or maybe even a king eider?" Both species were large, but if Murdock remembered correctly, eiders looked more like ducks than gulls. What he was looking at was far more gull-like than anything else. Was it an unusually big kittiwake, lost from its flock? Or maybe a fulmar. "Yes," Murdock decided. *That's gotta be a fulmar!*

Named for a foul-smelling, oily substance they can spray out of their mouths in self-defense, fulmars could fly very long distances. Murdock had never seen one up close. Excited, he thrust his powerful tail through the water and drew a bit nearer to shore.

The bird seemed to have taken an interest in the tilt-rotor parked on the beach. It took a few hops closer to *Red Tail*, its gaze clearly locked on the ramp and open door.

"Oh, no you don't," Murdock grumbled. He slipped below the water and picked up his pace.

By the time he resurfaced, much nearer the shore, the fulmar was perched on the aircraft's rampway, peering inside.

"Hey!" Murdock yelled, hoping to frighten it off. He spouted salt water from his blowhole for good measure. "Get away from there!"

The large seabird glanced toward the commotion Murdock was making. It studied the narwhal for a moment, then turned back toward the doorframe of the aircraft.

"I'm not kidding, Big Bird!" Murdock warned. "Don't make me go over there."

Murdock was easily fifty meters away still. Understandably, the bird did not see the giant marine mammal out beyond the breaking waves as much of a threat. It hopped inside and away from view.

"It's gonna be like that, huh?" Murdock slapped the

water with his long tusk, the equivalent for him of Arief pounding his chest.

With a well-trained muscle twitch, he toggled his barnacle radio on. "Team, we've got issues. You should have closed the cockpit!"

"What do you mean? What kind of issues? Have humans arrived?" The pangolin's tone was suddenly on high alert.

"A bird just invaded *Red Tail*!" Murdock complained.

A substantial silence followed the announcement. "A bird?" Wan finally asked.

"Yeah!" Murdock yelled. "It's in there now. It's a fulmar, I think."

This was supposed to worry Wangari, but clearly it didn't. "So?" the pangolin complained back.

"They're smelly!" argued Murdock. "Cranky too. What if it poops all over the controls?"

"Murdock, we're busy," Wan returned after another exasperated silence. "Just deal with it, okay?"

Murdock sputtered his growing frustration. "Fine. Murdock out." He gawked, stewing, as the bird waddled around within *Red Tail*'s interior.

Watching the waves build, Murdock mustered all his energy. The swell came at him, and he pushed off the wave just as it broke, surfing toward shore at top speed.

Beaching himself as a calf was what got him netted and shipped off to the Ark. But going hyper wasn't just a process that changed an animal's mind. Each of the Endangereds had also gained more control of their bodies, allowing them to move in new and more highly skilled ways.

Murdock braced for impact. He skidded to a halt against the pebbly beach like a boat running aground.

"Scat!" he commanded to the bird. *Maybe that's not the best choice of words*, Murdock thought. Scat was the official biologist term for wildlife poop, after all. "Go on! Git!" he insisted instead.

The large seabird continued to ignore the narwhal.

"That's it. I've had it." Determined, Murdock began to squirm his way up the embankment like a morbidly obese seal with a spear through its head. "Not on my beach. Nobody snubs a narwhal and gets away with it!"

CHAPTER SEVEN

ARIEF
(Pongo abelii)

Arief's feet and knuckles were numb with cold. But he pressed on, forcing himself to keep up with Nukilik. She disappeared over the ridge, and Arief quickened his pace, eyeing a bare, rocky outcropping where he might rest and give his hands and feet time to warm up.

When he reached the high ground, Arief was surprised to find half a dozen polar bears scattered along the landscape, all of them too thin. Nukilik cautiously approached the nearest of her kind. Arief posted up on the rocky landing and watched, happy to remain a healthy distance away.

Wan hopped from Arief's back onto the rocks and tested the breeze to determine which direction their scents were drifting. "Is this making you nervous at all?" she asked.

"They all look very hungry," Arief answered, breathing warm air into his cupped hands. "Let's try to stay downwind."

"Good idea."

"I am Nukilik," Nuk explained to the first polar bear she came to. Positioned at the top of a snowy knoll, it was alert and had a guarded posture. "I am the daughter of Atiqtalik. Have you seen her?"

"Go away," the polar bear answered, looking off in another direction.

"We were separated, and I was taken away from her."

"You are not of our gathering," the male polar bear insisted. "You are not invited to hunt here."

Gathering? Nuk thought curiously. But she understood why the sleuth had formed. When the ice is thick, polar bears wander far and wide with no specific territory, but as the ice melts and bears return to coastal areas to scavenge, they can find themselves in tighter groups.

"My claim to this place is older than yours." Nukilik's voice was deeply throated.

"We are here. The Ways are affirmed. Are you challenging us?"

Arief tensed upon the rock. "This is going nowhere fast," he mentioned to the pangolin.

Wan stood up on her hind legs and unholstered her single-charge taser prod.

"Hmmm," Arief murmured skeptically, eying the pangolin's tiny electric weapon. "Did you ever get a chance to test that on something as big as a bear? It might just make this fellow angrier."

Wan didn't look so confident. "But it's all I've got," she admitted.

Over on the small hill, Nukilik stifled a low growl and started over. It was plain to Arief that she was struggling to contain her frustration. "I am only looking for Atiqtalik. Do you have any information about her?"

"You are one against many. Go," the other bear answered with finality. He turned away.

"Can you at least tell me if you have encountered

others? How long ago did your gathering form? Did you drive other bears away?"

The sentry snapped back, his features broadcasting contempt. "You smell like human things. You move like a fox. You are not a polar bear."

Nukilik retreated several steps. Arief thought she might rear up in a sudden rage, but she lowered her head instead.

Arief's heart filled with sympathy.

Meanwhile, Nukilik attempted to circle around the sentry to approach the next nearest polar bear. The sentry bounded over and came between them. He rose on his two back legs for a moment, in a show of force, and then crashed heavily back to the snow. "Go!" he demanded.

Nukilik gave up. She shared a defeated glance with Arief and returned to where he and Wan were waiting.

Arief could think of no way to reassure Nuk. He remained still and quiet, offering her only a sympathetic sigh.

"Did you catch all of that?" the polar bear asked her friends.

"The dialect was thick," Wangari admitted. "But I think it all made sense."

"I would crush him in a fight," she eventually said. "But it would be unfair."

The orangutan nodded. "You're right."

She blinked away tears. "This is my home. And the home of my mother. They have no rightful claim."

"Everything has changed," Wangari pointed out, repeating what Nuk already knew.

"They're unhappy," the polar bear said. "I remember feeling the same confusion, about the betrayal of The Ways. . . ."

Arief felt his shoulders tighten. Wasn't this exactly what he had been worried about? It made sense that Nuk was having a hard time being patient. "Going hyper can be a curse as well as an opportunity. I'm sorry for what you have lost, Nukilik. And for all that you have learned that you cannot share with your kind."

"I could stay. I could lead them," Nuk said.

If Nuk decided to stay here, then Arief had no right to interfere. He didn't know what to tell her.

The hairs on Nukilik's back rose. Her eyes dilated. "Behind me! Now!" she shouted at her friends, stretching tall on her back legs.

Wangari instantly dove into a plated ball and rolled between Nukilik's feet. Arief wasn't that fast. He turned to see what the sudden commotion was about, and what he saw nearly stopped his heart.

A snarling polar bear bounded nearer, its eyes targeting Arief.

Instinct and training took over. The orangutan's muscles sprang into motion, and he cartwheeled to the side out of the polar bear's path. Nukilik stormed forward to occupy Arief's spot and met the attacker head-on. Both polar bears reared up, baring teeth and claws.

Arief backed away on all fours, his eyes glued to the battle. His breath caught in his dry throat. The scene before him was terrifying. The ground shook. He'd never witnessed an assault involving such bulk and so much pure muscle power. *She's deadly*, Arief thought with a shudder.

Nukilik was stronger, far sturdier than her half-starved opponent, but the assailant was mad with hunger and locked in on Arief. The bear ignored Nukilik and made another move toward the orangutan.

Seized with the kind of terror that only an unwitting

meal can suddenly experience, Arief tasted adrenaline in his mouth, but he slipped on the snow as he scrambled away. He lifted a forearm defensively and prepared for death.

But Nukilik was there and shoved the foe away.

"Stop it!" Nukilik roared, putting herself in the way of the next strike. "You're attacking my friend."

The weaker bear shook snow from its shoulders. It glanced away from Arief and studied Nuk. It sniffed at the air, and the crazed look in its eyes began to fade.

"Nukilik?" the polar bear asked.

"Yes, Mamma," Nukilik said, her voice on the edge of trembling. "It's me. I'm here."

CHAPTER EIGHT

MURDOCK
(Monodon monoceros)

Is this really *worth the effort?* Murdock asked himself as he trudged his way up the shore to *Red Tail*'s closed back ramp. He was exhausted by the effort and only halfway there. The beach rocks were polished but painful against his belly. Murdock prided himself for not dwelling on the past, but he was batting away flashbacks of when he had been beached as a calf.

"Tactical training," he grunted to motivate himself. "You want to go on the jobs, this is the price."

Even if the annoying bird wasn't trespassing in their

aircraft or threatening to ruin sensitive instrumentation, Murdock needed to get better at coming ashore. It might prove useful or necessary during missions.

"No pain, no gain!" he rallied, dragging himself another several meters forward.

At least no one was around to watch. He imagined the beached whale jokes Wan or Nukilik might spout off if they saw this.

"Quit laying around on the job, Murdock!"

"Long time, no sea, eh, Murdock?"

He was close enough to the tilt-rotor now that he could hear the bird moving around over the surf. "Get out of there!" he hollered again.

Wings flapped. The unseen animal released an impatient hiss as if it were telling Murdock to scram.

"That's it. I'm gonna impale you," Murdock promised. "Bird kabob." He swung his tusk with precision at the latch that controlled the cargo bay door. The belly of *Red Tail* opened. The narwhal executed a full doggy roll to align himself with the big ramp and started inchworming his way inside.

He slithered through his empty tank, tapped a fin on the touch light display within, and the forward glass panel slid upward, providing Murdock unhindered access to the cabin.

The large bird standing upon the captain's chair looked backward to find a narwhal creeping up on it and started coughing. It squawked anxiously while trying to right itself, then hopped back up onto the dash.

Murdock watched with fascination as the bird navigated the computer controls with a sequence of beak pecks that seemed rather . . . deliberate.

"HEY! Knock that off!" The narwhal rattled his tusk at the animal. "Fly, you fool!" Murdock cried for good measure, lifting his tusk high enough that he tapped the ceiling with it.

The bird fled for the side opening. It reached the ramp and immediately caught a strong gust of salty breeze and vanished with a final squawk of contempt.

Was that thing trying to type *something out?* Murdock wondered. It was a preposterous idea, and he dismissed it out of fin.

"Mission accomplished," he snorted proudly.

The narwhal glanced around as well as he could, slowly coming to the realization that he might be stuck now. He had no prayer of turning around in the aircraft's narrow tail section.

He had definitely improved at crawling forward . . . but backing out of here?

You can't let the others find you like this! he warned himself.

After Murdock punched some commands into his touch screen interface, the side door of *Red Tail* closed, and Murdock began experimenting with his tail, using it like a backhoe to scoot himself down the cargo ramp in reverse.

CHAPTER NINE

NUKILIK
(Ursus maritimus)

"Mamma, you're alive!" Nukilik exclaimed. She gulped back a sob and took a step closer to her mother. She smelled like . . . home.

Atiqtalik lifted her snout, and they touched noses. "Nukilik. I thought you had drowned." She brushed against her daughter and nuzzled her again. She cried out in relief, then circled Nukilik again, licking her neck and shoulders. She used the side of her snout to wipe Nukilik's gathering tears away.

"I looked for you," Atiqtalik said. "I searched

everywhere. I feared that boat had knocked you into the forever sleep."

"No, Mamma. I'm here."

"It was not time yet for you to leave me."

"I didn't leave, Mamma. I was taken." Nukilik nuzzled her mother, rubbing Atiqtalik's shoulder with her snout. She could scarcely believe her fortune and realized only now how depressed she had been. She had been so worried her mother was dead. But Mamma was here. She smelled like warmth in the dead of winter.

"The humans took you," Atiqtalik surmised.

"Oh, Mamma, so much has happened, but I swore I would come back and find you, and I did. I'm just sorry it took so long."

Mother was skinny. Her face was long and exhausted. The pride she had always carried on her shoulders was gone, replaced with something Nukilik did not have a word for. She looked distracted and unfocused.

"Mamma, you look hungry. I can help you."

She gave Arief a hard glare.

They were so close to each other, and yet Nuk felt a gulf separating them. Atiqtalik stared hungrily again at Arief.

"These other animals are my friends," Nuk explained. "The world is so much bigger than the Great Realm. I can't wait to tell you all about it, Mamma."

"I do not understand. We are predators," Atiqtalik said, disappointed. She looked off at the ocean. "Other species cannot be our friends, Nukilik."

"Mamma, listen," Nukilik tried. "I was taken to an island very far away. I can understand so much more now. My body has changed too." She lifted a paw and demonstrated. "I can flex my paws and grip things. I can stay on my hind legs and walk if I want to."

Atiqtalik just hunched there staring at Nuk, clearly confused and maybe even a little frightened.

Nukilik ignored her mother's reaction. She pressed on, certain that if she just explained her adventures more, her mother would understand what she had experienced. She might even be proud.

"Mamma, you always used to tell me that I was supposed to have a great purpose, that I would make a difference. I'm doing that! My friends and I are saving other animals and helping species to survive in this world where The Ways are going awry. I can help you too."

"I don't need your help, Nukilik," Atiqtalik said. "I warned you to stay away from the humans, didn't I?"

Nukilik stopped short. Mother was right, after all: the only reason Nuk had been captured was that she had approached the camp of Dr. Fellows and her assistant, Mr. Gooding. She had sniffed their rations, eaten the food stored inside their tent. If Nukilik had avoided the camp that morning, the humans wouldn't have targeted her. She remembered the words that Mr. Gooding had spoken to her just before she had been tranquilized.

"Looks like you chose us, gal."

"But I was hungry, Mamma."

"So am I, Nukilik," Atiqtalik admonished. "But The Ways provide."

That hurt. Nukilik groped for the right words. "Let me help. I can help all of you, if you'll just trust me."

"I have survived on my own. You take your path. You are strong. I do not understand what has happened to you, and I will not follow . . . I cannot follow. I am glad you are safe, but you are grown up now and The Ways demand that we follow our separate paths."

"Mamma, no," Nukilik whispered. "Please let me help."

Atiqtalik offered her teary-eyed daughter one last

nuzzle with her snout, and then she turned away and walked back down the hill toward the bay.

"Nukilik, I'm sorry," Arief said gently.

Nuk fell onto her haunches and sat in the snow, holding back tears.

Her friends waited with her in silence for a long time, watching Nuk's mother slowly vanish behind a rise in a whitewashed hill.

Finally, Wan ventured, "Do you want some time? Or we can head back if you like. Up to you."

Nukilik blinked several times and zeroed in on the pangolin and the orangutan beside her. *I'm not alone*, she realized. *I have my new family.* "Let's go," she said, rising. "I think I'm done here. Mamma did what The Ways demanded of her."

Arief knuckle-walked over to Nukilik, crunching the snow, and put a long arm around the polar bear's broad shoulders. "She still loves you, you know."

"I know." Nukilik was quiet, and then she said, "She will be okay, but I want to do what we can for her while we're still here. Can we leave all of our rations behind?"

Arief arched an eyebrow thoughtfully. "That's fine, but will she eat them?"

Nukilik nodded confidently. "She is proud, but not to a fault. If we leave food in her path, she will find it and gorge on it until she has her fill."

"We'll do it," Arief agreed. "I wish we could do more. But sometimes even a small gesture can mean a lot."

They rose and made their way back to the landing site.

"You'll have to tell me more about your own mother, someday," Nukilik said to Arief. "And what happened to her and your brother."

"Hmm." The ape offered up a short, thoughtful grunt and committed to saying nothing.

Nukilik spotted *Red Tail*, a dark shadow against the snowy coast down below, and set her sights. As she walked, the heartache and heavy feeling in the pit of her stomach was still there. Nuk suspected it might never entirely leave.

Maybe it's the feeling that all curious and adventurous animals feel, Nukilik hoped, *when each of us finally strikes out on our own.*

CHAPTER TEN

WANGARI

(Phataginus tetradactyla)

Wangari rode down the snowy hill on Nukilik's neck as the great bear made her way back to *Red Tail*. She fancied herself for a moment as a legendary knight mounting her majestic steed—of course, she would never admit that out loud to Nuk's face.

When they reached *Red Tail*, Nukilik jerked to a halt. Murdock was laid out among the large polished rocks on the beach like a . . . well . . . like a beached whale. His tail was ten meters shy of the surf, and his tusk seemed to be jammed between two small boulders so that his head was stuck off kilter at an awkward angle. He was pinned in such a way that he couldn't see who was approaching.

"I really hope that's a polar bear, a pangolin, and an ape I hear coming," he said despondently. "And not a photographer for *National Geographic*."

"What's going on?" Wangari demanded. "Are you trying to evolve?"

"While you all were playing in the snow, I was busy defending—" Murdock halted abruptly. "Evolve—hey, that's a good one!" He grudgingly laughed. "That's not what I thought you'd say."

"What did you think we'd say?" Arief dared to ask.

"I don't know. 'Thank you' maybe!" Murdock barked. "I saved *Red Tail*, in case you care."

Wan and Nukilik and Arief all turned to inspect the tilt-rotor. They shared a confused look. To Wangari, *Red Tail* looked exactly the same as it had when they'd departed. And a glance out to sea revealed no obvious threats. "From what?" she asked. "A hole in the ozone layer?"

Murdock grunted elusively.

"Wait, you're not talking about that gull are you?" guessed Wan.

Murdock diverted the conversation. "How about a little help here, okay?"

"You smell just about ready to eat." Nukilik flipped over the larger of the two rocks that Murdock's tusk had gotten wedged between.

Murdock immediately started working his way back up the beach toward the cargo ramp. Wan was rather impressed watching him. In spite of his unfortunate setback, he seemed to be getting the hang of pushing himself along the ground.

"Did you find your mother, Nuk?" he managed while grunting with effort. "You're back sooner than I figured."

"I did," Nukilik said. She didn't elaborate.

"It went that well, huh?"

"Murdock," warned Arief.

The narwhal snagged the cargo ramp lever with the end of his tusk and gave it a flick. The ramp descended, and Murdock worked his way up and into his dry tank.

"He's ready for a fresh bath, I bet," noted Wan. "Let's

build that storage igloo and stock it up with rations while Murdock's tank fills."

Nukilik retrieved a coiled-up hose from its compartment, coupled it to the compressor, and ran the end of it out and down the beach into the ocean. A cloud of white bird feathers materialized as the hose rolled open.

Wan took notice. *That bird was making a mess of things, after all.*

"There's a big pile of bird poop on my seat!" grumbled Nukilik.

"After all that?" Murdock grumbled back. "I tried. Better be careful, Nuk. Fulmar scat has a nasty reputation."

"It's not a big deal," said the polar bear, wiping up the mess with a rag.

Inside *Red Tail*, Murdock's tank began to fill with fresh salt water.

They constructed a serviceable snow cave close to where Atiqtalik's footprints where plentiful and transferred *Red Tail*'s remaining dry goods into it. Included among the foodstuffs were stacked bricks of protein bars, tubs of electrolyte solutions, and ample stores of powdered ground fish product.

"You sure she'll find her way to these supplies?"

"If the need is great enough, she will," Nukilik said, satisfied with their work. "Thank you for your help. Even if the other bears find it, there is plenty to go around."

"That's what we're here for," Wan answered.

Back inside *Red Tail*, Arief was going through his preflight checklist. "How's our fuel?" he asked Wan. "Are we stopping in Nova Scotia again?"

Wan hopped into her seat and studied her dash displays. "Fuel looks good. Flight plan has us on a more direct route back to the Galápagos. There's an automated filling station around the Great Lakes. Let's aim for that. Hey . . ." She paused, tapping a glass console with her large digging claw. "What's this doing?"

"Warning light?" Arief asked, adjusting the fit of his onboard headset.

"No. It's the tracker for our sloth friend," Wan said. She double-checked what she was seeing, then opened a command terminal. Everything seemed to be working properly. She growled.

"What's wrong, Wan?" Nukilik asked.

"The sloth. According to my instruments, he's back inside the textile factory again."

"What?" spat Murdock. The narwhal stopped preening himself as fresh salt water filled his tank and consulted his own touch screen displays. "That whole mission was for nothing?"

Arief sighed. "I worried that might happen. Never would have expected it so soon, though. Did we check to make sure there wasn't already a tracker on him?" Arief asked Wan.

The pangolin threw up her arms. "No. But now I guess we should have."

Arief cleared his throat and thought in silence while the team waited. He nodded after a moment. "The work we do: it's never over. Clearly these humans are more determined than we thought. It's on the way home, more or less. We'll go back and get it right," he said. "While we're at it, we might as well get a closer look at what's going on there."

"Hold on," Wan said. She had fished out the fashion gala invitation from her utility harness pocket. "If we go now, we'll arrive right as the party is getting underway. When I rescued the sloth the first time, the factory was mostly empty—and the extraction was hard enough as it was."

Nukilik pulled up a calendar on her dash monitor. "The Ark is due for a human walk-through late *tomorrow*," she reminded them. "We need to be in our habs when Fellows pops over for an inspection. Our window to help the sloth is *now*."

Murdock added to Wangari's doubts. "I've heard about big fashion events. They spare no expense. Security will be high. That gala is going to be a three-ring circus, even without us real animals there."

"Wait a minute," Arief said. "*'Even without us real animals there . . .'* Let me see that."

Wangari passed him the masquerade ball invitation.

The orangutan studied the invite and then nodded, a smile appearing at the corners of his lips. "Set a course for Panama," he instructed Nukilik. "I have a plan."

CHAPTER ELEVEN

ARIEF
(Pongo abelii)

Bahia Azul, Panama

The outer walls of the ruins were no obstacle for Arief and Wangari. Tall and thick and sturdy in some places, the ancient perimeter was crumbling and collapsed in others. The Endangereds infiltrated toward the rear of the factory compounds, where the ancient stones were overtaken by the jungle.

"Watch for a trip wire," Wan urged. "There's a cable here somewhere. I saw it running the length of the entire perimeter last time, so it must be back here too."

"Found it," Arief said. He braced the small leather

satchel looped over his shoulder. He effortlessly climbed partway up a tree trunk and swung himself to ground beyond the sensor wire. Wan ducked under the cable without slowing.

"We're in," Arief whispered into his hot mic.

"Copy," returned Nukilik's voice, *Red Tail*'s propellers whirring in the radio background. Arief could also hear the faint drone of the tilt-rotor in his naked ear. It hovered high above the canopy, a couple thousand feet overhead. "This infrared scanner is pretty handy! I've confirmed your heat signatures crossing the line. There's a ton of wildlife in the trees around you. But I'm not picking up any dogs on patrol in the courtyards. And the humans appear to be mostly inside or on the grounds near the glass-covered atrium, over."

"Copy that," Arief answered.

It was evening, not yet full dark. The air was humid but cooled by a gentle breeze. The gala was well underway at this point. In spite of a growing chorus of insect noises and frog song, Arief could clearly hear the murmur of human voices mixed with live music.

Wangari knew the layout of this place, but now Arief was getting his first close look. An old Spanish fort built over the top of ancient ruins, the compound had multiple modern wings and factory warehouses. Grassy lawns connected the grounds. The stone ballcourt, where the sloth's cage had been and where the fashion show would occur, was in the atrium between the factory's main offices and another building.

"Are you two sure you wouldn't rather wait until the party's over, cut a hole in that glass roof, drop down the rope ladder, and run a rapid extraction?" Murdock asked again.

Arief shook his head. "We've waited long enough. It's a good plan. Let's stick to it." He hoped his voice sounded self-assured. A good plan? Maybe. Daring? Definitely. It could go wrong in so many ways. . . .

"Whatever you say, Chief," Murdock replied. "It's your pelts on the line, not mine."

"You don't have a pelt, ice brain," Wangari said.

"Yes, I do!" the narwhal insisted.

"You have to have hair to have a pelt."

"All mammals have hair," Murdock explained. "And I'm a mammal. Order: Artiodactyla. Family: Monodontidae. So there."

Wan turned to Arief. "Is that true?"

"I believe so, yes," the orangutan said.

"If you have hair, where is it?" challenged the pangolin.

"Everywhere!" shouted the narwhal. "They're just . . . sparse," he said defensively. "Leave me alone."

"Time to focus," Arief insisted.

"The path is clear," Nukilik reported.

Arief and Wan immediately set off across the quiet lawn and advanced toward the cheerful sounds of the gala, keeping tight against the building walls. Wangari bounded ahead to scout, while Arief deliberately took his time and practiced walking fully upright. Straightening his back while stretching his legs was uncomfortable, but for short bursts, he was able to do it and maintain his balance.

"Arief, don't wave your arms like that while you walk," Wan warned. "You look like an ape."

Arief shot his arms to his sides and suddenly found it more difficult to press forward without swaying. "Walk like a human," he scolded himself. "I need to practice more back at the Ark."

"You're doing great," Wan reassured him.

They came to the corner of the factory's front entrance. From here they could peek around and grab their first good look at the gala attendees. There were a lot of humans milling about, hiding behind elaborate animal-themed costumes and masks. Almost everyone had a drink in hand and stood talking in small groups. A pack of human kids stood huddled within a white party tent. This event was, after all, a celebration of a new line of children's luxury outdoor clothing. A string quartet played music on a patio by the lobby doors, drowning out the chatter and the laughter and the sounds of the jungle.

"It's now or never," Arief told Wan. He pulled a bandit mask and a black bow tie out of the small satchel and fitted them to his face and neck. "It *is* a good plan, right?"

"They're all drinking and distracted by food and music," Wan said as she fished through the satchel herself, pulling out her own costume. "The plan will work."

Arief watched with growing doubt as the pangolin climbed into a makeshift poodle costume that she and Nukilik had designed on the long flight over. In the outfit made of cotton balls and patches of Nukilik's fur, Wangari didn't look so much like a poodle as she did a bleached racoon wearing a dingy bath mat.

Arief kept his doubts to himself, though; the team looked up to him, and he needed to project confidence.

Wan wiggled her prosthetic poodle snout into position. She clipped the end of a leash to the collar around her neck and handed the other end to Arief. "Time to take your prize pedigree for a stroll."

Arief adjusted his bow tie and took a deep breath. "You mean pound puppy, right?"

Wan gave him a confident wink. "Tell them I'm an extremely exclusive breed and they will all be very impressed."

"You're one of a kind, Wangari. There's no arguing that."

Wangari initiated her final preparation, stabbing a plastic spike with a small antenna into the grass lawn. She flicked a switch, and a green light blinked on, arming the high-frequency sonic pulse emitter.

Satisfied with the placement of the booby trap, she looked up at the ape. "Will you join me at the ball, darling?"

"I would be delighted," Arief said with a smile.

The orangutan, disguised as a human disguised as an orangutan, took a deep breath and stepped out into the courtyard filled with humans.

CHAPTER TWELVE

NUKILIK
(Ursus maritimus)

"They've engaged the crowd," Nukilik reported to Murdock. "The mission is a go."

"I see that," the narwhal snarked from his touch screens over in his tank. "I've got the same sensor readings as you."

They were listening to the ground team's radio signals but had turned off their own mics. Judging by the infrared imaging, brief glimpses through hacked security cameras, and the loudness of the cello solo in her ear, Nuk figured Arief was fully committed to masquerading as a costumed human at this point.

The ruse seemed to be working.

"You owe me a fish," Nuk said. They had made a friendly wager with each other, based on how long it would take before Arief and Wan's cover was blown. Murdock had guessed it would take ten seconds.

"Clearly the humans are more self-absorbed than I thought. We should find a place to land if this thing is going to play out the long way."

"Yup," said Nukilik. "Let's touch down nearby."

She zoomed out and recalibrated the heat sensitivity on the imager, scanning for a quiet clearing in the jungle where she could park *Red Tail*—somewhere close, though, just in case things went sideways and an emergency extraction was needed.

"Hold on," Murdock advised. "Zoom back in on the lower quadrant. Do you see that?"

Nukilik panned to where Murdock had indicated. Several humans were grouped at the loading docks behind the main factory building. Something about how they were clustered so far away from the party felt . . . suspicious.

"Can you pick them up on the visible spectrum?" Murdock asked.

"I'll try." She switched her feed to the optical scope mounted on the tilt-rotor's belly. They were in luck. Factory floodlights clearly indicated that the humans were loading drums into cargo trucks.

"What do you think they're up to?" Murdock asked. "Seems kind of hush-hush, doesn't it?"

"They look like they're up to no good," Nukilik agreed. "But it could also be nothing. They might be the caterers for the gala, or another delivery service."

Murdock was skeptical. "None of that explains why they'd be wheeling a bunch of fifty-five-gallon drums *into* trucks. I have to say," he added heavily, "the human fashion industry is a major polluter."

"I don't get this whole fashion thing," Nukilik admitted.

"Why would you?" said Murdock. "Look at that beautiful coat of fur you have! But humans don't like to run around without clothing. They're always covering up. And they like to be fancy about it too. That's why Chaz Devine is throwing this party tonight. He wants his clothes to seem cool, but what a lot of people don't get is that fashion is often terrible for the environment. While there are some companies making a real effort to be eco-conscience, the fashion industry as a whole is responsible for ten percent of global carbon emissions, pollutes rivers, puts micro-plastics into the ocean, and more. It's one of the bigger environmental problems that most people don't know about."

"Murdock, you're lecturing," Nukilik said. "What about those vats? What's the connection?"

"The bottom line is, a whale's worth of chemicals are needed to make most fancy human clothing. Dyes and bleaches . . . all sorts of toxic goo . . . It's also expensive to get rid of those toxic chemicals. If I was a betting whale, I'd bet my blubber that a big illegal dump is about to go down."

Nukilik was squeezing her paws together. Her jaw was extra tight. "We need to stop them."

The loading dock workers had finished shoving dozens of big drums into the delivery trucks. They were dispersing now. Drivers were jumping behind steering wheels while companions doubled up in passenger seats. The trucks pulled out of the loading bay and processed in single file around the buildings onto the main access road, pausing briefly at the first of two gatehouses controlled by factory security.

"Hang on," Murdock chuckled. "I want to test something. Tell me: which way are those trucks going to turn?"

Nukilik rolled her eyes. "Not now, Murdock. Seriously."

"No, I wanna see! Guess."

The polar bear growled. But she thought about it, really trying to discern whether the trucks below would take a right or left turn at the T-intersection in the jungle ahead of them. To the right were some of the nearby towns that had lots of hidden watery channels. The road to the left was less populated, but the shores of the bay were more exposed to detection from boaters on the open water.

"They'll go left," she finally decided.

All three trucks turned right.

"That's incredible," scoffed Murdock. "You're still batting zero!"

Nukilik didn't want to hear about it. She flipped on her comm. "Orange leader, come in."

"What is it?" Arief grumbled in a low whisper.

"We think this company might be doing illegal dumping. Delivery trucks full of factory materials are pulling off the premises as I speak."

Arief answered with a gruff "Follow them, if that's what you're asking. We've got things under control on our end."

"Copy that. Over and out." Nuk switched off her comm and refocused her attention on the trucks filing onto a dirt road. She switched *Red Tail* from hover mode over to manual control. "Let's find out what these humans are up to."

CHAPTER THIRTEEN

ARIEF
(Pongo abelii)

The orangutan and the pangolin walked openly among the humans.

It was an interesting sensation for Arief. Just like that, they weren't spying on the party—they were part of it.

"Keep acting like you belong," Arief reminded her. "If you believe it, they will too. We're on our own, now; the mobile team is following a lead."

"I heard," Wangari whispered above the live classical music.

They pressed forward toward the main factory steps. The kids in the pavilion tent were having fun pointing out each other's clothing and posing with friends for a photographer. Arief paused his gaze on one of them. He recognized the girl. She was famous, but he couldn't remember her name. He almost turned on his head cam to ask Murdock who it was—he would know—but he was interrupted.

"Oh my God. That's the best costume of the night. Who are you wearing?"

It took the ape a second to realize the woman approaching on the pathway was talking to him.

"Excuse me?" Arief managed, suddenly panicked.

"It's a fashion industry phrase," Wan quickly explained before the lady grew too near. "She wants to know the designer of your outfit."

He couldn't help a curt bark of laughter. "Natural selection," he replied with a smile.

The woman overheard him. "Natural Selection? I don't know that brand," she said. "I need to look them up. That fur seems so real!" She was wearing an acrylic masquerade cover with bright scales. As she drew close, she switched her glass of wine to her other hand and stroked Arief's arm. "Feels a bit coarse, though. Going for authenticity, I see. Is the designer here tonight? I must pay them my compliments."

"I . . . made this," Arief answered her.

"Absolutely marvelous. Even when you talk . . . the mask is so lifelike!" She giggled. "This evening is just wonderful, isn't it?" She held an unsteady hand up to her lips and burped. "Excuse me." She grinned sheepishly and trotted off, waving delightedly toward an arriving friend.

"That went well!" Wan commented. "Our disguises are working! Keep it up. Let's get through those doors."

The factory lobby was guarded by attendants checking for invitations. The Endangereds might need more than luck to get past them. "Be ready with that sonic distraction," Arief warned.

"That girl over there," Wan said, "with the curly red hair wearing the bear ears. That's Brianna Lennox."

"I thought I recognized her."

"Famous American pop singer. She also has her own TV show."

"How do you know that?"

The ugly poodle shrugged. "I hang out with Murdock too much."

Arief noticed that Brianna was missing part of one leg and wore a skirt and low-healed hiking boots that didn't fully conceal her prosthesis. For an event that seemed to Arief so focused on appearances, he had to give her credit for not covering her difference up.

"What is someone like her doing at a party with endangered sloths?" Arief wondered.

A young man blocked their path. His eyes were covered by a purple peacock mask. They widened with amazement, and he spoke loudly. "That. Is. A *genius* Wookiee costume! Who's it by? Tell me it's not the same guy who made Chewbacca." The man acted like he was afraid the answer might be yes, but then he laughed. "Seriously, though. Bravo!"

The man let out a woeful growl and laughed at himself. Then he glanced downward, saw the pangolin wearing glued-on cotton balls and polar bear fur, and startled. "Oh." He touched a hand to his heart. "That's . . . Well, what a brave little . . . *dog* . . . you have." He gave Arief an ashamed wince and hurried away.

"Woof you," Wan muttered.

"These people are very odd," Arief told Wan. "They don't care who I am. They just want to know about my 'outfit.'" He put air quotes around the last word.

"Try asking the next person who *they're* wearing," Wan suggested.

"I'm afraid we'll find out they're wearing a distant relative," Arief grumbled.

The orangutan was getting impatient. He figured it was best to wait until a line formed at the entrance before daring to dart past the attendants, but every minute they lingered outside they risked someone taking too much interest in them.

Another woman approached. She wasn't wearing a mask, but she was made up to look like a tropical bird. Arief stiffened his arching back.

"This is heavenly," she stated, giving his arm a gentle rub. "I must know who you're wearing."

Arief offered his practiced answer. "Natural Selection." Before she could ask more, he interrupted her with a question of his own. "Tell me," he said. "Do I know you?"

"Oh, I'm sure you know *of* me." She laughed, flattered. "I'm Hailey. Hailey Rigatoni. Owner and CEO of a little something called . . . Rigatoni Cosmetics?"

Arief got the sense that he should act like he knew what that was, so he did. "Oh, hi!"

"It's okay. The costume is confusing people," she admitted, looking at him through intriguing contact lenses patterned after reptilian eyes. "I know you'll ask, so I'll just tell you: I'm wearing myself. The makeup is from my brand-new line of exotics. I can't say much without revealing a billion-dollar secret recipe." She winked and laughed showily. "But it looks so lifelike and supple because, well, we don't mess around when it comes to *authentic* ingredients." She winked at him again.

Gross, Arief thought. He felt his hands ball into fists. *She's talking about animal products. . . .*

Wan brushed against Arief's leg, possibly sensing his building anger. "Just focus on getting inside," she urged, trying to make it sound like a dog bark.

"Oh, look at that adorable dog." Rigatoni sighed. "I love that you love rescue pets!"

Arief watched as Wan's expression tightened angrily, then relaxed again, as if with effort.

"Rigatoni Cosmetics long ago cornered the market on skin paints. But we're reaching new heights with these updated makeups. Would you like to enter with me?" she asked Arief abruptly. "I've been playing this game all evening, trying to figure out just who's who under the best costumes. And you've got me stumped so far."

Arief cast his dog an arched eyebrow. *We may not need a distraction, after all.*

Sensing his best opportunity to slip inside unnoticed, Arief shoved his outrage down deep and gave the lady a smile and a nod. "You'll have a hard time guessing who I am," he promised her.

"I love a good challenge," she said excitedly. He withheld a groan and let her take him by the elbow.

They joined the loose line of partygoers waiting to enter the indoor portion of the gala.

"Let's see," Ms. Rigatoni started in. "Are you in entertainment?"

"Tell me more about your wardrobe," Arief suggested instead.

The cosmetics CEO took the bait. "I thought you'd never ask!" she began.

She rambled on, and the line advanced. The nearest guard looked quite impressed by the quality of Arief's getup. Unfortunately, he was eyeing the orangutan awfully hard. "Invitation?" he asked gruffly.

Annoyed, Rigatoni waved the guard off like she was shooing a fly. "He's with me."

Arief glanced down at Wan and nodded.

"I'm sorry, ma'am, I still need to see his—"

Two nearby guard dogs started to bark and whine and pull at their leashes. Arief caught Wan winking up at him as she pocketed the clicker that had triggered the sonic pulse. He could hear distant ringing, but the emitter had been set specifically to a dog's higher range of hearing and was clearly more of a nuisance for the canines than it was for Arief or Wan.

The doorman abandoned Hailey Rigatoni and her guest without a thought, rushing to the aid of the inconsolable dogs. It was the cosmetics queen who tugged at Arief's shoulder, taking advantage of the moment. "The gall of that guy. Come on."

And just like that, the ape and the pangolin were escorted inside the factory like VIPs.

They passed into the large glass atrium bridging two of the factory buildings, where the ancient ballcourt was festooned with elegant party decorations and fancy lighting. A stage dominated the far corner of the space, and final preparations were underway for the start of the evening's official fashion event. The sloth's cage was still at the far end of the court, but the sloth wasn't on display.

Instead, he was being passed around by partygoers over by a photo studio set against large stone artifacts.

"They're getting pictures taken with him!" Arief said under his breath, disgusted.

Arief assessed the tactical situation. It was pretty clear that the path of least resistance to retrieve the sloth was for him to wait in line for his turn at a photo—then make their escape.

Hailey Rigatoni chatted on and on before finally wrapping up. "I need a bathroom. I'll leave you here for now. But come find me later!" she insisted. She leaned in and pecked Arief on the cheek before he could react. "So lifelike!" she remarked again, exhilarated. Then she stepped lively toward the nearest exit.

"Thank the figs," sighed Arief. "I was beginning to think we'd have to call in an emergency extraction— just to escape her."

The pangolin chuckled in response. "I should get going."

The orangutan knelt down, pretending to adjust Wan's collar. "You're ditching me?"

Wan spoke quickly. "I remember where the security room is from my earlier op. If the airborne team is really onto something shady, I can find out more about it from there."

Arief nodded along. "And meanwhile I'll wait here in line for my turn with the sloth. If you're in the control room, you can conjure up a distraction when it's my turn."

Wan winked. "That's my specialty, boss."

He unbuckled her leash, and the pangolin scurried off.

"Oh, your dog's running off!" exclaimed the masked lady in line in front of him, sloshing her drink.

"It's fine," Arief explained dismissively. "She's well-trained."

He smiled to himself. *In the art of espionage, that is.*

A lone man made his way down the line toward Arief, engaging in small talk with each group of guests. Tall and broad shouldered, he had a trim, graying beard and wore a gorilla suit under a tuxedo. He wore no mask, and Arief recognized him from his research as the lead fashion designer and CEO of Scenic Trails, the clothing brand hosting the fashion show tonight.

The human reached Arief and put out a hand. "Good evening. I'm Chaz Devine."

Arief met his strong grip. They stood awkwardly locked in a handshake battle until Devine pulled away.

"And you are . . . ?" the CEO pressed when Arief offered no greeting.

Arief teased him. "It's a masquerade ball, remember? But I'll give you a hint. I'm a big investor, and I'm going all in on the rarest clothing lines."

"Well, your money is well spent on our portfolio," the CEO assured him. "Your costume. The coat looks *so* real," he continued. "Is it?"

Arief guarded his expression and admitted grimly, "It is."

Disgustingly, Chaz Devine seemed impressed. "I do love authenticity. Well, you've put my gorilla costume to shame. I hope you're enjoying yourself? Our models will be showcasing the new line starting any minute."

"I got a glimpse of Brianna Lennox outside," Arief said.

"Pretty cool, right? We're excited to be joining forces. She's a big influencer! She loves the outdoors too. Having her join with us will do wonders for sales."

"Are those clothes really meant to be worn while hiking and camping?" Arief asked.

"Are you kidding?" scoffed Devine. "Our clothes are too expensive to actually take camping. Campfire smoke lingers in fabrics for weeks! It's more the look we're going for, wholesome outdoor adventure. Honestly, I couldn't care less about camping, or nature for that matter, unless it makes me—and our investors—money. Why do you think we moved our headquarters here? It's so much easier for us to stay ahead of the environmental regulations."

"Oh, really?" Arief growled. *That explains what Nukilik and Murdock have stumbled onto.* He got to thinking: *I wonder how much this blabbering baboon will confess to.*

He reached up a hand to rub his temple, while discreetly pressing record on the head cam hidden beside his bandit eye mask. "How interesting. Can you say more?"

CHAPTER FOURTEEN

WANGARI
(Phataginus tetradactyla)

Wan dashed upstairs, timing her sprints for when she was sure all eyes were focused elsewhere. Knowing the building's layout, and without the security systems armed, she found the effort a breeze.

Until she got to the top of the grand staircase, that is.

Out of the shadows halfway down the long corridor, a rottweiler sprang to its feet.

With fangs bared and ears folded back, it launched itself at the pangolin.

Wangari froze. It was unlike her to freeze. But then again, it was unlike her to be weighed down in an ugly poodle costume. By the time she could react, the dog was almost upon her. She curled up, losing control of the clicker for the sonic pulse. It slid over the edge of the stairs. She felt the mist of the rottweiler's breath before the dog skidded to a halt, yelping in pain.

Wan dared a glimpse. It had reached the end of its chain leash.

She uncoiled herself. Luckily for the pangolin, the control room was in the opposite direction down the hallway. "We can play fetch later," she told the dog, her words drowned by its barks and growls.

Wan hightailed it down the corridor, but as she got to it, the door to the control room burst open suddenly. Wangari dove for cover. She rolled behind a tall planter in a nook just in time to avoid detection by the angry guard wanting to know what the ruckus was about.

"Chiquito. ¡*Callate!* What's the matter, huh? Chiqui, it's okay!"

The dog fought its leash with all its might, to no avail. Its eyes never left Wan's throat. The human strode toward Chiquito.

As soon as the human passed, Wan bounded to the control room and quietly closed the door.

The room full of computer screens was empty of people now. *Thanks, Chiqui,* she thought. *That worked out nicely.* She listened while the guard tried to make sense of the dog's agitation. One of the radios on the countertop sounded. "Martín, what's up with the dog up there? He's bothering the guests."

"He's worked up. I'll take him outside just as soon as I'm sure it won't cost me a hand."

"Well, hurry up about it."

Wan caught her breath. She had the room to herself for at least a few minutes. With a leap she locked the door from the inside and scampered up onto the guard's swivel chair.

"I'm in," Wan reported into her open mic. "Give me a minute to orient."

Arief didn't answer, but that was fine. She could see on one of the monitors exactly where the great ape was in line for the sloth. He was speaking to . . . another great ape—this one a handsome middle-aged man disguised as a silverback gorilla.

She grabbed a keyboard and started prying into the

computer systems. Within a moment she figured out what to do. "Arief, I've got a lot of levers I can pull here. You want me to choose?"

Arief faked a cough while whispering a reply. "Whatever you think is best. Wait until it's my turn with the sloth, then work your magic."

Perfect, Wan thought. The problem was, though, she realized, it might not be Arief's turn at the front of the line for a good ten minutes. Martín might be back before then.

"*Red Tail* to ground team, over," Nukilik's voice rang unexpectedly in Wan's ears.

"I copy," Wan said. "Arief can't talk much right now, but he's listening."

"The trucks are heading down a dead-end road toward a hidden estuary," she reported. "Murdock is convinced they're going to dump toxins there."

"They can't get away with that." Estuaries were areas where fresh water from the land met ocean salt water. They were full of wildlife and particularly fragile to pollution.

"Can you get any more intel on their plan?" Nukilik asked.

"Gimme a minute," Wan announced. "I can jack into the drivers' radios. I'll listen in for clues." She moved a dial on the consoles in front of her, eventually patching into audio feeds of the delivery van drivers. Jackpot. The drivers were talking up a storm. They were on their final approach to the site and planning to ditch the vats of dye ahead of a factory inspection tomorrow.

Wan reported what she'd heard to the others while simultaneously patching coordinates of the dumping site over to Murdock.

Murdock shared his outrage. "This calls for action. We're going in."

Arief gave them the green light, in spite of the danger this created for himself. He spoke into the radio using a hoarse whisper. "The CEO is admitting to me what they're doing. Unbelievable. We have to stop them. It's a risk we're going to have to take."

The doorknob to the control room rattled. Wan's gaze darted toward the window just in time to see a human form looming in the hallway, holding out keys. "I have to go. I've got company!"

Wan jumped out of the chair, leaving it spinning. But when the guard stepped back into the small room, he closed the door quickly and locked it. Wan had no way to scurry out unseen. Instead, she backed into the shadows beneath a countertop and crouched there, uncertain what to do next.

CHAPTER FIFTEEN

MURDOCK
(Monodon monoceros)

Murdock and Nuk arrived at the estuary and found the end of the road, where brackish water was lapping up against the mangroves. Murdock had splashed down into the swamp, and Nukilik had landed *Red Tail* nearby. It was immediately apparent to the narwhal that someone had been dumping harmful chemicals here. Metal drums of varying sizes were littered everywhere: on shore, bobbing on the water, caught in gnarled mangrove roots, sunken and half-buried in silt. All of them were rusty, dented, or cracked. A lot of the drums clearly hadn't been sealed and their toxic contents had bled into the bay. Murdock could taste the poor quality of the murky water as he braved the inlet where the road ended.

The damage already done . . . This is an outrage. . . .

The coastal swamp was noisy with the chatter of insects and frogs. Murdock slid his belly along the muck and surfaced, unheard, amid a patchwork of aquatic plants.

Nukilik was merely a silhouette against the darker silhouette of trees. She trudged over to Murdock's position, huffing gruffly as she labored through the bog. "The mud!" she grumbled. "This stuffy tropical air! The water's so warm. And the bugs! So many bugs!"

"Nothing tops our top of the world," Murdock sympathized. "But the tropics have their charms. The squid around here can be pretty tasty."

Nukilik snorted. "Are they coming to this inlet or not?"

The narwhal gently touched the broad length of his tusk to the shore for a moment. "I can feel vehicles approaching. It's the transports," he confirmed. "Be ready."

"Amazing," Nuk offered. "How does that work?"

"Evolution, I guess. My tusk is great at sensing vibrations in the water," Murdock boasted. "Hard to explain. Think of it as an antenna."

"What are we going to do when they arrive?" Nukilik pressed. "What's our plan?"

"Aren't you the rampage-first, plan-later gal?" Murdock teased.

"Look at this!" Nuk ignored her partner and batted at an empty steel drum stuck in the mud. "What a mess. I'm just going to eat the jerks who did this."

"Maybe we should try something less homicidal first," Murdock suggested.

Something surfaced in the water nearby, catching Murdock's attention. There were no lights out here, but Murdock guessed by the sounds it made as it left the water that it was a sea turtle.

"Nuk. There's a turtle coming ashore. Nab it, will you?"

"A turd?" the polar bear asked. "Murdock!"

Murdock vented brackish water from his blow hole. "No! I didn't . . . A TUR-TLE, you albino reindeer. A sea turtle. This polluted cove is no place for it, whatever species it is."

"What do you want me to do with it?" Nuk wondered.

"I dunno. Put it in *Red Tail* for now?"

Nukilik positioned herself to intercept, but the hard-to-see creature submerged before beaching and vanished for good.

"It's all on you, now," Nuk pointed out. Murdock squirmed backward a few tusk lengths, ready to track the animal down, but Nukilik stopped him. "They're coming."

Just then the trees began to glow with sweeping vehicle headlights—several pairs. Only a moment later the narwhal glimpsed the white cargo hold of a large delivery truck approaching through the thick mangroves.

"What was that plan of yours again?" Murdock gulped.

"We didn't get very far," Nukilik admitted. "I think we were at 'Try not to eat any of them, at least not right away.'"

"Well, that's a start! I say we improvise."

"Huh?"

"Make it up as we go."

"Now you're speaking my language." Nukilik

punched on her headset mic. "Wan," she urged. "You copy? We have confirmation. We're about to engage, over."

Neither Wan nor Arief offered a reply.

Three big delivery trucks pulled into view and turned around at the end of the narrow road. The nearest of them started backing down the muddy rampway.

Nukilik stomped farther into the shadows while Murdock sank beneath the water.

Shark Week cometh early this year, my lovelies, the narwhal thought with a smug jet of bubbled laughter.

CHAPTER SIXTEEN

ARIEF
(Pongo abelii)

"And therefore," Chaz Devine was explaining, "fewer regulations are the only way to make a killer profit. We're only delivering what our investors demand: big margins! Everyone has to keep up with the latest trends, right?"

"But you say you're eco-friendly," Arief countered.

"That's marketing for you." Chaz took another sip of the drink in his gorilla-gloved hand. "We *are* eco-friendly. *Economy*-friendly. See? Down here in the swamps no one's watching. We can bend the rules and turn a profit."

"Not to mention a nice salary for yourself," Arief said with a sarcastic smile.

"Hey, why not? It was my idea to relocate to Panama. Dumping our dyes and hiring cheap labor has boosted our margins."

Arief drew in a long, patient breath. He didn't dare avert his eyes from the Scenic Trails CEO's face; his head cam had Devine framed front and center, so there could be no confusion who was saying what. "What about Brianna. Does she know?"

"Bri-Len? She has no idea. Those influencers are all alike; they don't ask uncomfortable questions. What she doesn't know won't hurt her." Chaz took another sip of his beverage.

"You're almost up!" the CEO said before giving Arief a powerful pat on the shoulder and then mockingly knuckle-thumping his chest and grunting like a fellow great ape. "Enjoy the sloth. I ought to mingle, but here's my card if you're serious about investing."

Disgusted, Arief glanced away and focused on the sloth, who was surrounded by a fawning group of women. The orangutan was next in line for a pic. He and the CEO must have chatted for ten minutes! He thought back over the conversation, realizing just how much damaging information he had secured. But he ground his teeth as he turned off the recording. What was he supposed to do with the footage? Would the humans around the world even care if this conversation got out? And who could he even hand the evidence over to without blowing his cover?

The women were starting to fight over who would get to hold the sloth for their group portrait, and they were getting a bit rough with the animal.

Arief growled through pursed lips. *Your first job is to get the sloth out of here.*

But what about the diversion that would allow him and the sloth to slip away?

"Wan?"

Arief surveyed the ballcourt and the pace of his heartbeat picked up. He had scarcely registered the guards at the doors and all around the room. He couldn't dodge them all without a grand fake-out. Furthermore, dozens of guests were still waiting in line for a photo with the sloth.

"Wan, come in. We need that distraction asap."

No answer.

Wan's last words from the control room echoed ominously in his head: *"I've got company!"*

"Wan, if you can hear me, I'll be ready for sloth removal any second now, over."

Still nothing.

Arief shifted his weight nervously from one foot to the other.

At the far end of the glass-covered atrium, the fashion show was getting underway. The theme was rustic and rugged. It was a fusion of rain forest and steampunk elements, as several large industrial sewing devices were set up as props among the jungle palms and hanging vines.

Brianna Lennox was at the edge of the constructed runway, emceeing the glitzy affair with other children dressed in Scenic Trails outfits behind her. They launched into a song-and-dance number. Arief wanted to plug his ears against the noise. *Those kids are being used*, he thought angrily. *If only they knew how offensive all this is.*

"Bri-Len, Bri-Len, Bri-Len!"

The animal-costumed crowd cheered and the lighting inside the factory refocused on the runway.

Can I snatch the little guy away now? Arief wondered. But there were still folks waiting in line for their sloth picture. The fashion show alone wasn't a big enough distraction.

"Hello there!" the photographer called over. "You're up!"

Arief started, jostled out of his concentrated state. His apprehension bloomed. "Wan!" he hissed into his hidden comm.

But again, there was no answer.

CHAPTER SEVENTEEN

MURDOCK
(Monodon monoceros)

Beep, beep, beep.

The first of the big trucks backed down the final stretch of road to where the dirt gave way to lapping estuary water. The bright red brake lights illuminated the inlet, so that Murdock was forced to submerge to avoid detection. The backup beeping ceased. He watched through rippling water as a couple of humans lifted the rolltop door of the delivery vehicle, revealing twenty or so fifty-five-gallon drums stacked within.

Murdock surfaced for a clearer look just beyond the

reach of the lights. He scanned the banks for a polar bear but failed to spot Nukilik.

Oh, she's out there, Murdock knew. *Crouched in wait like a white ninja.* His considerable stomach churned with something like glee. *This is going to be fun.*

Speaking broken Spanish to his workers, the American foreman extended a ramp from the truck and hopped into the interior. The team worked fast in the dim light provided by the trucks. The first of the heavy barrels rolled down into the water with big splashes. Murdock tracked each one, watching to make sure their lids were sufficiently sealed and that the drums weren't about to sink or leak.

So far, so good, but they were barreling down the ramp fast, and it would only take one loose lid to make a disaster. . . .

"Nuk, what are you waiting for?" Murdock said aloud.

The answer came fast.

The truck buckled and rocked suddenly. A scream emanated from the cabin, and then the polar bear materialized on top of the vehicle. She swiped a paw down hard on the rolling door's locking mechanism.

116

The door fell like a guillotine. A barrel blocked it from slicing a worker in two.

"Albino jaguar!" shouted the American foreman, terrified.

"*¡Chupacabra!*" someone else yelled from the darkness.

"*No. ¡Es Ulak!*" another cried. "Bigfoot!"

Murdock slapped the water with a fin, a form of marine cheering. The workers suddenly noticed the large sea monster and screamed again.

The polar bear dropped heavily to the ground beside a man; she gave him a stern look, but didn't attack.

"Please, don't eat me. I'm sorry."

"No more polluting," the polar bear commanded, snarling. She was mostly a silhouette among the tall ferns, but her eyes and her fangs glowed red against the truck's back lights. Murdock could imagine the humans believing what they were seeing was some kind of supernatural spirit. He snorted laughter.

"No more!" the man vowed, sobbing. "They pay us to do it, but I know it's wrong. My family lives near here. *We're* the ones who suffer because of the factory."

Nukilik turned toward the front of the truck and

bounded out to where the foreman cowered. "Find a new line of work!" roared the polar bear.

"I quit!" hollered the American, sprinting down the road for his life.

Murdock listened as the rest of the vehicles peeled away. The workers nearest the shore chased after their friends on foot, leaving the half-empty delivery truck behind at the water's edge.

Within seconds, the jungle was quiet again. Nukilik sauntered back into view and grinned brightly in the red lamplight. Covered in so much mud, she resembled a terrifying lagoon creature. "That wasn't so hard."

"I didn't even get to skewer anyone," Murdock lamented, sliding up close to Nuk. He offered the polar bear a high "one" with his tusk.

Nukilik gave the narwhal's pointy end a triumphant tap. "Gather all these drums at the ramp," she suggested. "I'll roll them into the truck. Let's clean up around here."

"You bet," Murdock agreed. "I'll collect the older trash scattered around too."

Murdock got straight to work, hunting down the barrels bobbing about in the inlet. He nudged them toward the ramp using his tusk, and rounded up older, deteriorated drums along the way.

While submerged in the muck, he flushed a sea turtle from hiding. He realized it was the same turtle he had seen before. In the light, he saw that it had a severely damaged front flipper. It was also missing an eye. *Poor thing.* The narwhal half followed it, half chased it to shore. It pushed up onto a coarse, sandy embankment and glanced back at Murdock with an expression that seemed to convey annoyance.

"Hey, don't give me that look," Murdock told it. "You need to get out of here. Take your buddies, if you have any, and go. We're cleaning up as best we can, but this area may be polluted."

Right then a huge gull swooped overhead. It landed beside the turtle and retrieved something long and mechanical hidden in the grass, then placed it at the turtle's side. Lost in the dark shadows, Murdock couldn't make out what it was.

The gull twitched violently and coughed, seized with fits. Murdock looked on in growing astonishment as the large bird regurgitated a . . . cigarette lighter.

"Dude," Murdock exclaimed. "Did you just hack up a plastic lighter?"

"Not my fault," the bird squawked hoarsely. "Some fish ate it first. How was I supposed to know a lighter was in its g-u-u-u-u-u-t?" It finished with a long, involuntary belch.

Fascinating as that was, Murdock wasn't in the mood for a whole conversation. There were still drums bobbing in the inlet. "Go on, get out of here," he told both animals. "I've had enough of seabirds," he added. And then he thought of something. "Hey, what species are you anyway?"

"Alba-a-a-a-a-atro-o-o-os," the bird struggled to say. It coughed again, then twitched again. "Albatross," it repeated, this time more clearly.

"I saw someone as big as you way up north just this morning," Murdock muttered. "You guys closely related to fulmars?"

"No idea," the albatross quacked. "What's a . . . a . . . fulma-a-a-a-a-a-r?" The bird jerked again, hacked a few times, and spit something new out of its beak. It looked like a button.

What happened next was a total surprise.

The sea turtle stood up on its hind flippers. It lurched

for something hidden in the reeds and scooped it up with its good front flipper.

"Whoa. Wait." Murdock gurgle-gasped.

With a practiced movement, the turtle fitted the device onto its deformed flipper and somehow tightened it into place. It was a prosthetic fin, and it had various contraptions folded into the end.

Murdock couldn't believe what he was seeing. He couldn't believe what he was about to say. "Wait a minute. You guys are . . ."

The turtle looped a black eye patch over its head, covering its deformed eye socket.

". . . hyper!" Murdock managed to spit the word out.

"What's hyper mean?" asked the albatross, its throat finally clear.

The sea turtle nodded while adjusting its eye patch. "We're here to protect the bay too, broseph," it admitted. "We're hoping you'll help *us*."

Murdock stared at the two creatures in shock, for the first time in a long time at a total loss for words.

CHAPTER EIGHTEEN

WANGARI
(Phataginus tetradactyla)

Wangari crouched in the far corner of the security control room under the U-shaped counter, hiding from the guard who had just sat down in front of the computers. She had a good angle on several of the monitors showing camera feeds. One of them displayed a high-vantage perspective of the portrait studio by the sloth's cage.

It was Arief's turn in front of the photographer.

The sloth was hanging from Arief's neck, and the orangutan kept putting his free hand up to adjust his bandit mask, or more accurately the radio headset hidden beneath it. Wan watched as his simian lips formed her name in desperation over and over. She had turned off her earbud audio entirely, afraid the guard in the room might detect even the smallest, tinny whisper from it. But she didn't have to hear Arief to know what he needed.

It's time, Wan knew. *Arief's counting on me.*

She eyed the switches midway up the far console. A few flips of various levers, and the party would be ruined. Problem was, the guard was inconveniently seated directly in front of the control panel.

I'm going to have to nerve-pinch him, she concluded.

Wan wasn't enthusiastic about the idea. Dropping humans out cold rarely worked. And even when it did, the victim usually came around within seconds—not minutes—of falling flat. Furthermore, the door to the security room was locked, offering Wan no easy escape.

None of this mattered, of course; Arief and the sloth needed her *now*.

Wangari crept out of hiding. With the guard's back facing her, she scaled the desk against the far wall and secured her footing on top of the counterspace. She was level with the control switches now, just on the wrong side of the room. She tiptoed across the U-shaped counter at a steady pace, hoping to avoid catching the guard's attentive gaze as he studied the monitors spread out before him.

Her eyes were locked on her target—and she missed what was right in front of her. She kicked over his cup of coffee! Hot liquid spilled across the counter, scalding the guard's arm. The mug fell to the floor and shattered. The guard jolted and cursed. He glanced in Wan's direction and then yelped.

Both Wan and the guard froze.

"What the hell are you?" he finally managed. Wan thought about what she must look like to the startled human. Her dog costume was falling apart. She'd removed the fake nose long ago. The guard stared, half-mortified, half-fascinated, before lifting a walkie-talkie to his mouth. "Jacobs, I know why Chiquito was freaking out earlier. We've got a diseased anteater on the loose here."

The handheld radio burped with confusion. "Huh?"

Now. Wangari leaped from her position on the counter, digging claws out, and landed on the guard's shoulder. She wrapped her long, scaly tail around his face and executed a forceful nerve chop to his jugular. The same move had once collapsed Nukilik to the ground, so she was hopeful it would buy her a moment now.

The guard cried out, convulsed, and slid limply from his chair. But Wan came with him. Before she could untangle her tail from around his neck, her head struck the edge of the counter.

Wangari blacked out.

CHAPTER NINETEEN

MURDOCK
(Monodon monoceros)

"Nukilik! You've got to get over here!" Murdock trumpeted. "Come see, quick! These animals are hyper!" The polar bear was on the far side of the inlet, trudging through the dark mud as she rolled old barrels up onto dry land.

"What's hyper mean?" the tall white bird asked again.

"You're extra smart!" Murdock exclaimed. "Like a human. Or even smarter, really."

"Ah . . . yeah, we don't call it hyper," the sea turtle

explained, fidgeting with one of the accessories on his bionic appendage. There was an arc of electricity, and then a soft light came on at the tip. "We call it going brainy."

The albatross twitched suddenly, lurched forward, and coughed up a disposable contact lens. Grossed out at himself, he gagged, tripped, and got one of his webbed feet stuck in the mud. A frenzy of flapping followed.

"Some of us are brainier than others," the one-eyed sea turtle chuckled.

"Hyper, brainy, whatever." Murdock laughed. "And you're a bird and a reptile! I was starting to wonder if it only happened to mammals. This is incredible news. We should totally join forces. My name is Murdock, and the polar bear is Nukilik. What are your names?"

Before either of the brainies could answer, Murdock shouted out again, "Nuk! Get over here!" Then he turned his attention back to the newcomers. "Sorry. Go on."

"I'm Honu," said the sea turtle. Murdock studied him more closely. Honu was a green sea turtle. Scientific name: *Chelonia mydas*. But there were two distinct subspecies of green sea turtles, if the narwhal remembered correctly: Pacific greens and Atlantic greens. Atlantic greens tended to have browner shells with splashes of other colors showing up in the pattern. Honu's shell was a dark, dark green—almost black in places, and his belly plate was distinctly green. This was more typical of the Pacific subspecies.

"You're a Pacific turtle, aren't you?" he asked pointedly.

Honu gave his partner a knowing look, then answered, "I am. I'm Hawaiian, actually."

"What are you doing in the Caribbean?"

"What are *you* doing in the Caribbean?" the turtle snapped back.

Murdock was surprised by the turtle's tone.

"I am MAR!" shouted the albatross, startling Murdock and Honu both.

"And I am hearing you just fine," Murdock scolded the bird. He would have rubbed his earholes if he could reach them. He backed away, and his perspective of Mar shifted. "No way," he said to himself.

Is it possible? The theory that had suddenly lodged itself in Murdock's blubbery noggin couldn't be true, but he couldn't shake it, all the same.

"Was that you?" he demanded from the bird. "In the Arctic? In our plane?"

The bird and the turtle shared another look. Mar seemed to grow more uncomfortable than usual. He cocked his head but didn't answer right away.

Murdock was growing more convinced of his theory every second. "I can't believe it. It *was* you. I thought it was a fulmar, or some other large *arctic* bird. But it was *you*."

"I got stuck on your plane after you freed the sloth," Mar confessed rapidly. "You tried to get rid of me, but I wasn't going to be abandoned in that place. . . . I stowed away again for the ride home."

"I knew it!" the narwhal crowed. "But . . . why?"

"I was scoping you all out, to see if we should recruit you. I didn't realize your next stop would be the North Pole!"

A bit of mist spurted from Murdock's blowhole. A very muddy Nukilik strolled into the turtle's sphere of light. Taken suddenly aback, Mar squawked his alarm and took flight.

"Why am I doing all the work?" Nukilik grumbled.

"And you're over here beaching yourself again."

"Nuk! These two animals are hyper! Or brainy. Or whatever."

Nukilik studied the sea turtle with the Swiss Army flipper standing upright between them. "So, not all sea turtles stand upright like that?"

Honu activated his flipper's taser function in protest. A blue electric arc crackled menacingly for a moment. "Nope. Just me, broseph. Just me."

"The bird is an albatross," Murdock explained. "Mar was stowed aboard *Red Tail* for the Arctic journey. He's the one I was trying to shoo away!"

"Wait," said Nukilik suspiciously. "We had a rogue hyper hiding and spying on us the whole trip?"

"They said they were scoping us out to see if we could help them with their operation," Murdock summarized.

"What operation?" Nukilik demanded. "Tell me how you got to be hyper."

"What's a—"

"It's the same as brainy! Now stop asking!" snapped Honu at the bird. The turtle turned back to the Endangereds and explained, "You'll have to learn to be patient with Mar. He's pretty screwed up, thanks to all the microplastics in his diet. The brainy thing didn't . . . fully . . . 'take,' we think."

"I don't care about that," insisted the polar bear. "Start explaining yourself. We have work to finish here. Any of these drums could crack open yet. And every minute we're here, we're not running point for Wan and Arief."

Murdock was a little taken aback, but he understood her impatience. "Will you help us finish loading this truck?" he asked the brainies.

"Finish?" asked Honu incredulously. "None of this is over yet. You're just going to rescue the sloth, put him back on the island again, load up these drums, and that's it?"

"That was the mission," Nukilik stated flatly. "We saw an opportunity to do more, and we took it. But we need to check in with our team before we improvise any further. Are you going to help us with the cleanup or not? I want all the drums that could still potentially leak packed away."

"Why stop there?" asked Mar pointedly. "Why not shut down that factory for good?"

"What do you mean?" said Murdock, intrigued. *Maybe they have a point,* he thought. There was no harm in hearing them out. . . .

Honu reached his good flipper into the shadows along the water's edge and retrieved a leather satchel that had apparently been hidden there. He held it up for show.

Murdock was partially shocked and totally infatuated. "Is that a bomb?" he exclaimed.

The green sea turtle nodded proudly.

Nukilik scoffed. "That's not how the Endangereds do things. We save those who need saving. We don't blow things up. No way. Innocent animals and people could get hurt, or worse. Now let's get these last barrels loaded up, Murdock, and get out of here." She stomped over the truck ramp and began shoving the drums collected at its base toward the cargo hold.

The albatross flew upward and landed on the top of the ramp, where he blocked Nuk's progress. Murdock couldn't get over how giant the bird was. Mar looked like he could give Nukilik an honest beating if he wanted to. "Stop right there, lady! Now you listen to me. I'm sick and tired of pooping plastic and coughing up toothbrushes. Everything I eat these days—fish, fish eggs, krill, squid, you name it—I always end up with more plastic in my gut. Everything I eat has already eaten human trash! And Honu . . . he lost the end of his flipper in a fishing net—and his eye to boat propellers. When does it stop? When do the humans learn their lesson? It's time to light the fires and fight the liars! So . . . are you with us, or what?"

"Move out of the way," Nukilik ordered.

"There's no time for arguments," Honu said.

"Scram!" Nukilik said to the bird, cautiously swatting at him. The albatross flew up on top of the truck. The polar bear proceeded up the ramp with the next barrel and moved deeper inside the truck to stack some drums to create more space.

Honu waddled over to the back of the truck, holding his utility appendage high. "Mar?" he prompted.

The albatross bent over and used his strong beak to release the pin holding up the rolling gate. It fell shut with a slam, trapping Nukilik inside.

"Hey!" yelled the polar bear, her voice angry but muffled. The truck shook, and Murdock imagined her stomping back toward the door with her claws flexed.

But before Nuk could yank the door up from the inside, Honu employed his electric arc tool as a welder. The metal latch fused with the floor of the truck bed.

"We'll show you the proper way to crash a party," Honu promised menacingly.

"What are you doing?" Murdock blasted. "No! Stop that!" He rushed the shore, scraping painfully up onto the gravel driveway, and continued flopping his way toward the crazy sea turtle.

Ironically, the turtle was too fast. He marched for the driver's side door before the narwhal could stab him. He lobbed the satchel into the cabin and hopped up inside.

Murdock slapped at the back door, testing its strength. No use. If Nukilik couldn't tear through it from the inside, his tusk wasn't going to make a dent.

The truck's ignition roared to life. "Get back here, Honu!" Murdock yelled, a wave of panic washing down his lengthy torso. "What are you going to do?"

The truck drove away, leaving Murdock in a cloud of dust.

CHAPTER TWENTY

ARIEF

(Pongo abelii)

"I've been eyeing you," said the photographer to Arief.

"Uh-oh," the great ape murmured, preparing for the worst.

"Really looking forward to snapping some pics of that costume!" the camera guy finished excitedly. "Do you mind if I take a few of just you before you hold the sloth?"

Arief relaxed and released an explosive sigh. "Wonderful idea," he answered, straightening his bow tie.

This buys me some time! He nodded good-naturedly and strode over between the ferns.

"Can you pose like a real orangutan? Hunch over, drag your arms a little?"

Arief obliged the photographer, who reacted with amazement. He was so excited that he started drawing the eyes of others around the stone ballcourt. "That's astonishing! Yes, do that! Oh. My. God. Hollywood called. They want their King Kong guy back."

Arief slouched, which only reinforced his natural form. *Not exactly avoiding attention here.*

"Okay, now beat your chest a few times," suggested the giddy photographer.

There were so many eyes on him, he didn't feel he could risk saying no. Instead, he rapped his knuckles against his breast, trying not make the motions too authentic-looking. The gesture was a silverback gorilla thing, anyway.

A crowd was gathering. Everyone laughed. Someone pulled out their smartphone.

Wan, where are you?

"Hey!" yelled the nearest guard, rushing over to the crowd. "No outside cameras allowed tonight! You're supposed to hand in all phones. Give it over."

Sulking, the offending partygoer relinquished his device to the security guy.

The photographer's assistant approached Arief with the sloth. "Here she is. Don't be nervous, she's harmless. Let her put her arms around you and don't forget to smile!"

He's a male, Arief wanted to snap at the man. But he scooped up the animal without a complaint and held him protectively.

The sloth slowly looked Arief in the eyes and gave him a tight hug. He buried his face in the orangutan's neck fur. "You're back," he whispered. "Please get me out of here."

The photographer was in the throes of ecstasy. "So precious. Hold that pose! Look, she's, like, *really* hugging him!"

"Twin cousins forever!" cooed a lady back in line.

"I'm here to get you home," Arief reassured the pygmy sloth quietly, throwing his voice through tightened lips.

"I'm sorry you had to return again," said the sloth. "They knew right where I was, and I couldn't get away."

Arief patted the small creature down and felt *two*

suspicious, cold lumps on its back. Either one of them could have been knots in the sloth's greenish fur, but he could tell by their regular shape that both were tracking devices. One of them was a creation of Wan's—and the other must belong to Chaz Devine. Arief cursed himself. "This won't happen to you again," he told the sloth. "I promise."

"Okay, one more pose, you camera hogs!" declared the photographer. "I need to get through the rest of this crowd before the fashion show ends!"

"Wan?" Arief grumbled into his comm.

The camera clicked several more times leaving Arief half-blinded by the flash.

"Please hand the sloth back to my assistant now," insisted the photographer. "I've got a ton of fab shots of you two. They'll be available for download in the morning."

"Can I get just a few more?" Arief tried, leaning on a knuckle while repositioning the sloth to his other shoulder. "Wan!" he pretended to cough.

"Hey, come on, man," complained the next human in line for a photo. "Move it along."

Arief glanced at the complainer, feeling a bit dazed.

Should he hand the sloth back over, then linger here, waiting for the right moment? Or make a break for it?

"Wan, come in!" he pleaded.

"I don't want to be stuck in this line for Bri-Len's entire performance!" protested someone else farther back. "Your turn's over."

"Please, sir, hand her back." The impatient assistant's arms were outstretched, waiting.

To make matters worse, the CEO was circling back around, eyeing Arief sternly. "*Amigo*, what's the grudge?" Chaz Devine's smile was forced and impatient. "Let's wrap it up. The show's happening."

"The little guy's really taken to me," Arief offered. "I think he's exhausted. Maybe he needs a break from all this."

"We'll take care of it," Chaz promised. "Come on. I'll escort you over to VIP seating myself."

Arief felt his posture growing defensive as the crowd, led by Chaz Devine, took a step toward him.

"I don't want trouble," Arief warned. "This little guy just needs a rest, that's all."

The CEO's expression darkened. "Who did you say you were again?" he asked pointedly.

"I didn't," Arief replied gruffly. "It's a masquerade ball."

"Hand over the sloth," Devine demanded.

Four security officers closed in, hands resting on holstered Tasers.

"Wan! Now or never!" Arief called out, loud enough for anyone to hear.

But there was still no answer.

CHAPTER TWENTY-ONE

NUKILIK
(Ursus maritimus)

As soon as the delivery truck jolted into motion, Nukilik was thrown off balance. She stumbled and slammed against the back door. Several of the stacked drums followed. The polar bear was hammered over and over again. Nukilik was pinned down by them, unable to move. And then when the transport hit a bump in the road, the loose drums shifted again and Nuk was able to muscle her way to greater wiggle room.

One of the drums had lost its lid, and Nukilik's lower half and left arm were doused with purple dye.

That can't be good, she thought angrily. She hoped her mud-caked skin was protected. She breathed chlorine gas and coughed.

"Here," Honu shouted back from the cabin. Something black was flung into the cargo hold.

Nukilik went to fish for it among the toppled barrels and took a good look at the front of the hold as she did so. A window with thick steel bars faced the back of the cabin, which opened onto the thin bench seat behind the driver's seat. The polar bear could easily reach a paw through the slats, but she wasn't sure she could stretch forward enough to swipe at the turtle behind the wheel.

Meanwhile, she found the object Honu had tossed back to her. It was a large gas mask. She immediately strapped it on. It wasn't a great fit, but her eyes stopped tearing, and if she breathed only through her snout, the burning in her throat ceased. She realized her headset was missing, knocked off by the drums at some point and buried somewhere in the back of the truck with her. She glanced around for it and saw nothing but toppled barrels.

"I'm not trying to kill you," Honu yelled. "Like I said: We want to partner up. We need more muscle."

Nukilik scrambled toward the grate. Another bump in the road bucked her, and she landed painfully against the lip of a rusty drum. She pressed on. "You've got a terrible way of selling the idea," she growled.

"I just don't take no for an answer, that's all."

Nukilik glanced through the bars and saw the turtle's satchel draped over the passenger bucket seat. It was within reach. Desperately, she lunged for it and yanked it back. The leather strap snapped like a rubber band, and she shimmied the bag through the bars and into her possession.

"What? No!" cried Honu, his gaze shifting front and back as he drove through the dark jungle. "Pass that up here!"

"Never," Nukilik promised. "Game over." She opened the flap and pulled out the bulky device within. It definitely looked like bad news: a nest of wires and cables meshed together with a circuit board and two transparent canisters filled with liquid, one clear and the other red. A tab was yanked loose from the housing when Nuk freed it all the way out of the bag, and a timer set for ten minutes started to count down, beeping with each change in digits.

"Game over, indeed," tsked the sea turtle. "Nukilik, you've gone and armed it! Now hand it back so I can reset it!"

"Not a chance, Honu! You can tell me how to deactivate it—or else we're all going up in flames together."

"Suit yourself," the one-eyed turtle answered, accelerating down the road toward the factory lights in the distance. "We're not dealing with a reasonable species out there. I'm blowing up that textile plant one way or the other. If you want to be stuck with the bomb when it goes *bang*, that's on you."

CHAPTER TWENTY-TWO

WANGARI
(Phataginus tetradactyla)

Wangari's vision was blurry. Her head stung. Something large stirred in her field of view.

It took her a moment of concentration, and then things started to make sense again.

I'm in the control room. I was fighting with the human. I hit my head.

The large, stirring object lying on the floor next to her came into focus. It was the guard. He was looking back at her with glassy eyes, blinking away his own confusion.

How long have we been out cold? she worried.

"Hand over the sloth." The CEO's voice was coming through the radio.

Wangari glanced up at the monitor with the security feeds. She saw Chaz Devine confronting Arief.

I have to do something!

Wan struggled to right herself and rise up off the floor. She rubbed her head. The countertop seemed miles away. But she needed to get up there.

On the monitor, four security officers closed in on Arief. . . .

"Hey, you . . . ," said the guard, coming around finally. He too rose onto all fours, on shaky limbs. He swiped a hand awkwardly at Wan. She dodged the attack.

"I don't have time for this," Wangari told the man, whose name was Martín, she now remembered. The pangolin darted forward and slapped him across the cheek with her open palm, hard.

"Ow!" said Martín. "What was that for?"

"Wan! Now or never!" Arief cried out across the radio waves.

Wangari took advantage of the guard's surprise.

She sprang onto his shoulder and then launched onto the counter.

"Get down from there!"

The angry warning went unnoticed. Wan found the lever she was looking for. She yanked it down.

"No! Not that one!" cried Martín. He was on his feet. He lunged at the pangolin and managed to grab her this time. "Oh my God, what have you done?" He pulled her back to the ground, hard. She rolled into a protective ball before slamming down on the tile floor.

But Martín's effort was too little, too late.

Wan dared a peek between her curled paws. On every video feed she could see, the glass-ceilinged heavens opened up and poured forth their pandemonium.

The sprinkler system had been activated.

Category-5 Hurricane Wangari was in full effect.

CHAPTER TWENTY-THREE

ARIEF
(Pongo abelii)

For the first time tonight, Arief feared for his own safety.

The CEO's eyes darkened. His expression turned menacing. "You're a saboteur, aren't you?"

A startling hissing noise emanated from above. Everyone looked up at once only to be met by a heavy downpour from the overhead sprinkler system.

The screaming started. People scattered like they were running for their lives, leaving behind feather boas, animal masks, shattered drink glasses, purses, clutches, even high-heeled shoes. Mascara bled down the cheeks of women and men both, rendering them into nightmarish racoons. Coats were soaked. Dresses were stained. One of the guests, wearing a particularly elegant salmon costume, with sparkling sequins for scales, tripped on an ancient stone curb and slid like a fresh delivery down the pathway. The hem of Hailey Rigatoni's expensive dress had snagged on a thorny planted bush. She sobbed in frustration as she struggled to free herself without tearing it.

The child models in their Scenic Trails outfits ran for cover, a few of them laughing while others cried out in alarm. Brianna Lennox stood still beside her microphone stand, arms crossed. She watched the unfolding madness with an annoyed—but also half-amused—expression.

Chaz Devine turned to Arief, while his security guards glanced around, whiplashed. They all shouted hurried instructions to each other at once.

Arief grinned brightly, blinking away the rain. It had only taken the span of a few heartbeats for chaos to engulf the party. *Wan, you came through!*

"Hold on tight," he warned the sloth, pushing the animal up onto his shoulder so he could ride piggyback.

Arief knuckle-sprinted toward the sloth cage. He leaped up and latched himself to the links with all four hands and feet and scaled to the top with ease. He ran along the roof of the cage and jumped for the stone side wall of the ancient ballcourt.

"Stop him!" Devine screamed. "He's stealing the sloth!"

But Arief didn't look back. He climbed up over the stone hoop protruding from the court's wall and ducked for cover. He glanced in all directions, gaming out his next move. His situation wasn't great. The structure he'd climbed onto was an island, for all practical purposes. The glass ceiling and its support beams were high out of reach. The string lights that drooped overhead wouldn't hold his weight if he tried to swing along them toward the exits. He was effectively marooned.

The sprinkler system abruptly shut off.

It took a beat longer for the screams and the moaning of the soaked guests to stop.

Great . . . there goes my distraction. Arief risked a peek over the low wall. Fleeing partygoers clogged the exit doors. Some of the kids were splashing puddles at each other, giggling. The guards were calling out orders, shouting over each other and wiping water from their eyes. Chaz Devine spun in circles, streams of dirty water dripping off his gorilla suit.

"Wan?" Arief radioed. "I'm not out of trouble yet."

"Copy. I know. Neither am I," replied the pangolin. "Just gimme . . . gah! . . . a . . . second." The sounds of a struggle commenced, with the unmistakable grunting of a human in the mix. There came an exasperated curse about an anteater, and then a groan. A couple of clangs and crashes later, the sprinklers resumed.

"That'll buy you a few more seconds," Wan reported. "But I can't keep this up. My buddy here won't stay down!"

"Copy," Arief grumbled, peeking over the high wall from his perch atop the ballcourt. Two guards were pacing at the foot of Arief's position. Two others stood at the court's center with weapons drawn. "Rendezvous at my location. I may need backup."

"Hold on a sec," Wan replied. "I have an idea. Let me just . . . activate this. . . ."

Arief didn't understand. He was about to ask for clarification when he saw a bunch of small metal pedals pop out of the ground along the ballcourt's stone floor.

A pacing guard triggered one of the levers by stepping on it, and a dart instantly appeared lodged in his pant leg. He cried out in pain, clutched at the dart, and then keeled over unconscious.

"Is that poisonous?" Arief asked Wan, worried.

"For me or a rat, sure. The human'll wake up with a headache and a sore ankle."

The other guards and Chaz Devine ran forward, eyeing Arief. Each stepped on the triggers along the way before they knew what they were doing.

Darts flew. The guards and their gorilla boss fell in a lazy heap.

"That'll do it for you," Wan quipped. "Mind the triggers on your way out."

"Brilliant." Arief smiled. He dropped down off the wall with a series of controlled falls, gripping edges of the stone blocks where he could. The sloth held tight around his neck. The sprinklers continued to douse the atrium and the stage. "Let's rendezvous outside instead, southeast courtyard."

"Copy. Just need to chop one more nerve core . . ." A loud slap, a grunt, and a heavy thud followed. "Yup. On my way. Over and out."

CHAPTER TWENTY-FOUR

NUKILIK
(Ursus maritimus)

Nuk glanced at the countdown display.

05:26

She'd wasted half her time already, fretting, searching among the spilled drums for her lost headset, and
trying without success to talk Honu down. But she
wasn't going to let the turtle have this bomb back. There
was still time to find a solution. . . . *Maybe I can just . . .
take it apart. Or smash the circuitry!*

Nukilik raised the bomb over her head, ready to hammer it down against one of the drums.

"Are you insane?" Honu cried, watching through the rearview. "It's tamper-proof. A short will detonate it. And if those two liquids touch because you shatter the tubes, the bomb will ignite anyway, ripping the truck open and showering the jungle with toxins for half a mile in every direction. It was supposed to go off *indoors*. And we were supposed to be long gone by the time it detonates."

Nukilik growled. She wouldn't hesitate to sacrifice her own life to stop this bomb from hurting others, but destroying the jungle for miles . . . to spare the *factory* from harm? There had to be another play. She would stall as long as she could.

05:02

Wan and Murdock will know how to defuse this thing. I need to fetch that headset! She glanced toward the back door and the drums piled up there. The headset was buried somewhere beneath all of it.

Cradling the bomb as carefully as she could, she scrambled over the strewn drums and used her free paw to dig. She caught sight of the radio and reached for it. It slid away when Honu turned sharply. Then it slid back in a wave of purple liquid. Nuk snatched at it and caught hold of it. She shook it dry, flicked it on, and talked into it without taking the time to fit it around her head and the gas mask. "Wan! I've got a ticking bomb. I need your—"

The delivery truck rammed through the first of two gatehouse checkpoints, splintering the wooden arm barricade to smithereens. Security agents and guard dogs scattered for safety. Another drum toppled over, slamming into the polar bear. Nukilik was splashed with large sloshes of blue dye, which overlapped some of the purple areas and covered more of her muddy white fur.

Nukilik was able to glimpse the road ahead through the slats and the windshield. Honu was driving toward a second barricaded gatehouse. Beyond, the old mission turned factory was lit up with festive lights, with some sort of automated light show flashing brightly through the glass walls of the big atrium. The glass-encased ballcourt and fashion show stage were swarming with costumed people and kid models. Almost everyone was running for the exits, soaking wet.

"Honu, stop! You'll kill everyone! What are you doing?"

"I'm carrying out my mission. I'm not playing around here." Honu adjusted the steering wheel, aiming the truck for the large glass wall encasing the ballcourt and stage. "We're reclaiming the wild!" he decreed. "We'll remember you, Sister Nukilik! You offer your life for a righteous cause!"

Honu jammed a stick down on the gas pedal. He opened the driver's side door—and flung himself gleefully out of the truck.

CHAPTER TWENTY-FIVE

ARIEF
(Pongo abelii)

Arief and Wan hid halfway up a tree in the jungle with the sloth clinging to the orangutan's neck. They were safe in the shadows. And they could retreat deeper into the overgrowth at a second's notice, should the dogs or the guards pick up their scent. Wan was back in possession of her harness and all its tools, which she had stashed at the base of the tree at the start of the operation. Arief was able to keep an eye on the factory from the hiding place. His view was partially blocked by the big white tent on the nearest lawn. He was amused but remained extra vigilant, remembering the outrage in the CEO's eyes.

Underestimating the humans had once cost him his entire family.

Arief had no doubts: when Chaz Devine awoke, pounding headache or not, he'd unleash every tool in his arsenal to get his trophy sloth back.

Arief would never let it come to that.

"There's the guard I fought with," Wan said, indicating a corner of the lawn by the dirt road that led away from the factory. The man was frowning while he limped painfully toward the gatehouse along the back perimeter of the compound. Far beyond the gatehouse, Arief glimpsed approaching headlights.

"He doesn't look happy," Arief chuckled. "Do you know if he got a good look at you?"

"Oh, he sure did." Wangari laughed. She was plucking the last cotton balls from any remaining sticky patches on her scales. "I attacked him and took him down three different times. He knew I was an animal. He heard me talk! But I don't think anyone will believe his story."

Arief allowed himself to laugh. "You mean he won't

report to his superiors that an African black-bellied pangolin disguised as a poodle incapacitated him in order to commandeer the factory's security to break an endangered sloth out of captivity?"

"Yeah. That. I don't think he'll report that to his superiors," Wangari agreed cheekily.

Arief and Wan's earpieces both chirped to life with sudden commotion.

First came Nukilik's cry for help: "Wan! I need help. I've got a ticking bomb—"

The narwhal's agitated blubbering cut off the polar bear. "We've got a code purple!" Murdock was screaming. "Code purple, over!"

"What's a code purple?" Wan asked.

Arief shook his head unhelpfully at Wan. "Worse than code red? I don't know—"

"Murdock, slow down," the pangolin urged. "What's going on?"

"Rogue hypers," Murdock cried. "Sea turtle and albatross. Kidnapped Nuk. Hijacked a transport. They're heading toward the party with a swimming pool's worth of toxic dye, a bomb . . . and a polar bear."

"What?" said Arief.

"They mean to hurt people."

"*Who?*" Arief demanded. "Murdock, you're not making any—"

"No time to explain. Just be ready. They're heading your way."

And as soon as the radio clicked off, the headlights he'd seen through the dark jungle a moment ago were visible again. A truck was racing down the long stretch of dirt road toward the factory's inner gatehouse at high speed. Poor Martín had to leap out of the way of the oncoming vehicle.

"*Wan! I've got a ticking bomb.*"

"*They mean to hurt people.*"

"Oh, no," Arief muttered.

"Boss." Wan cleared her throat. She had raised a pair of mini binocs over her eyes. "There's a one-eyed turtle driving that truck."

A hyper turtle? Arief thought. But there was no time. The truck was on a collision course for the inner gatehouse. And just beyond the gate, on the factory lawn hundreds of wet humans were milling about, including children.

The turtle flung itself from the vehicle and tumbled

into the brush as the truck continued to career forward.

"Stay here." Arief placed the sloth on a branch of the tree and started sliding down the trunk. "Go!" he shouted to Wan. "Get over there before someone gets killed!"

Wan leaped from tree to tree, branch to branch, as she descended to the jungle floor and tumbled onto the factory lawn. A wave of terror washed over Arief. He dropped to the ground and knuckle-galloped through the underbrush, knowing that—despite their best efforts—neither of them would reach the vehicle in time.

CHAPTER TWENTY-SIX

NUKILIK
(Ursus maritimus)

Driverless, the truck jostled over the uneven dirt road.

Nukilik gulped. Panic gripped her gut, but she pushed it all away.

Through the slats she had a good view out the front windshield. There was a crowd of people mulling about on the lawns and beneath the pavilion tent. None of the humans appeared to be aware that a large truck was speeding toward them. A truck loaded with explosives.

She looked down at the bomb she held in her paws, glanced around at the pile of fifty-five-gallon drums rattling all over. *One thing at a time*, she thought. She gripped the bomb protectively in her arms, then flung her weight at the far side of the cargo hold. The truck teetered but righted itself and continued forward.

She tried again, but this time she piled a few of the barrels up against the same side of the truck first. She rocked and threw her bulk high along the wall. The extra stacked weight made the difference. Seconds away from the glass atrium, the truck tilted on its right wheels, balanced there on edge for a moment, and then fell on its side.

Nukilik, twenty steel drums, and several hundred gallons of toxic fluids were instantly weightless. The polar bear strained against the forces buffeting her. She cradled the bomb to her chest, curled into a floating fetal position, and braced for impact.

CHAPTER TWENTY-SEVEN

WANGARI
(Phataginus tetradactyla)

The pangolin sprang out of her dive roll and bounded like a greyhound toward the path of the oncoming delivery truck. As light on her feet as she was, she knew she wouldn't make it across the lawn to intercept it in time.

But the stakes were too high not to try *something*.

The vehicle blew past her, balanced on two wheels. It teetered and finally tumbled, pitching forward onto its nose. It slammed against the ground and tumbled again, coming to rest on its side within meters of striking the building.

"Nukilik!" cried Wangari. *She's going to be badly hurt!*

"There's a bomb!" Arief shouted from somewhere behind her. "Go! Run! Get out of here!" His voice carried, and the humans heard him. They met chaos with chaos. Screams rose from everywhere all at once. Partygoers ran from the lawns, making for the outer exits in a panicked stream. Wan caught hold of the orangutan's silhouette as he dashed toward something.

The pangolin bounded for the truck, her every thought focused on Nuk.

Did she survive that crash?

Is the bomb still ticking?

So when the attack came from above, she hadn't seen it coming at all.

CHAPTER TWENTY-EIGHT

ARIEF

(Pongo abelii)

Arief watched as Wangari raced to Nukilik's aid. "There's a bomb!" he yelled at the crowd of people with all the power his lungs could muster. "Go! Run! Get out of here!"

He spied the guard over by the gatehouse, the one who had fought with Wangari in the control room. Arief barked instructions at him: "Radio your people in there! Evacuate the grounds. There are men who may need assistance, including Devine."

Wide-eyed, the guard snatched up his radio and called for help. Meanwhile, the crowds stampeded toward the broken barricade of the gatehouse.

Arief spied the turtle. He was struggling to climb the outer stone wall, using an artificial "ice-pick" arm to hoist himself up. He saw his chance and hot-knuckled toward the reptile.

If the critter made it over the wall and slipped into the jungle, he'd likely disappear forever. Arief couldn't allow that to happen. He needed answers.

He reached the wall and climbed it with ease, grasping for the turtle's nearest flipper. With a firm yank backward, Arief pulled the animal to the ground and he landed awkwardly on his back. Arief jumped down beside him.

"What are you doing?" he shouted, struggling to turn over. "We only have seconds to get away. The blast will kill us if we're in the open like this!"

A stab of mortal fear ran up Arief's hunched back. Arief put a foot down on the turtle's plastron, the belly side of his shell. "Then tell me how to shut it down!"

"Never," the one-eyed turtle spat. "How can you

even *think* of helping these criminals? Humans—they're all polluters. Murderers. A virus upon the earth. You're just prolonging their rule over our planet!"

"You're not going to solve anything with violence," Arief insisted.

"You wanna bet?" cried the turtle. Its appendage suddenly crackled with blue electric flame. It whipped its modified flipper up and connected with the orangutan's gut.

Arief flew backward twenty feet and fell to the ground.

He patted down his stomach, stamping out a patch of hair that was catching fire. When he was finally able to sit up and take a proper breath, he glanced toward the turtle in time to see him slip over the ancient wall and dive out of reach.

CHAPTER TWENTY-NINE

WANGARI
(Phataginus tetradactyla)

The assault upon Wangari arrived like a meteor strike. The pangolin's heart nearly stopped. A raptor attack had always been one of Wangari's most dreaded natural fears, and now it was happening!

Knocked flat, Wan instinctively curled into a protective ball. She patted her softer underbelly with her tucked-in claws for any signs of damage. No cuts or blood. *That's lucky*, she thought. She clutched the micro-Taser fastened to her harness. It had one charge to it; she would have to make it count. She sprang out of her tight scaly ball and thrust her weapon at where she sensed the raptor was looming.

A flash of electricity lit up the courtyard. There was a hellacious squawk, a cloud of downy white feathers. When the debris cleared, Wangari was surprised to find, gasping for breath, an enormous, twitching . . . *seagull*?

"Aa-a-a-a-aah-hegck!" It writhed painfully, making something like a grass angel on the lawn. It choked worrisomely, then coughed up a half-digested green toy soldier. "What a wo-o-o-o-orld!" it wailed up at the stars.

Murdock had mentioned an albatross. It made no sense, but then, the rogue sea turtle didn't make any sense either. Wan didn't have time to sort through it all.

She left the giant seabird behind and dashed for the toppled delivery vehicle.

"Nukilik!" she cried, circling the truck in search of a way in. The loading door was somehow *welded* closed. The passenger door was pinned against the ground, and the driver door was buckled and jammed shut. The windshield was shattered into a spiderweb pattern and impenetrable. Wan climbed through the missing driver window and immediately saw the slats opening into the cargo hold. The bars were too tightly spaced for her to pass through, and the view was blocked by a wall of dented steel drums. Her eyes teared involuntarily, and she backed away. The chlorine gases wafting through the slats were intense. "Nukilik!" Wangari cried again, fearing the worst.

There was movement within. Wan heard a groan. It was the polar bear! *Thank the ancestors.* "Nuk! You okay?"

"I'm pinned down!" Nukilik answered, her voice under heavy strain. It sounded like she was wearing a mask. "Wan! I'm still holding the bomb. There's only two minutes left. Get as far away as you can. Evacuate everyone!"

"What kind of bomb is it?" Wangari demanded.

"It has two liquids. If they mix, it'll blow. Honu said it was strong enough to make a crater out of the whole region."

Wangari searched her mind, holding panic at bay. There was no point in running, even if she had chosen to abandon her friend, which she would never do. "How many wires are there?"

"There's a ton of wiring."

"But look for the power source. How many wires run between the battery and the liquid canisters?"

"There's two," Nukilik answered.

"That's fantastic! You want to pull out the negative cable. But *don't* disturb the positive. The positive is probably red."

"They're both dyed purple. Everything's purple."

Oh, no. No, no, no.

Wangari's relief was instantly replaced with utter dread. *Fifty-fifty chance*, she thought. *Crap!*

But they were out of options. What else could they do?

"Nukilik," she said as calmly as she could. "I can't get to you! You're not going to like this, but you've got fifty-fifty odds. You're just going to have to pick one wire or the other."

CHAPTER THIRTY

NUKILIK
(Ursus maritimus)

"WHAT!?"

"Pick one," Wan urged.

I can't do this! Nukilik despaired. *I'll pick the wrong wire! I always make the wrong choice!*

She was hunched over, her knees and her nose pressed to the ground. Her headset had fallen away again during the crash.

She could hear a dreary moan rising throughout her cramped quarters, wondered if it might be Murdock radioing, and then she realized it was coming from her own throat. The bomb had two wires that were the same width, and both were now dyed the same color.

Which one was she supposed to disconnect?

"Nuk? You've got this!" Wangari encouraged her.

"Shut up and let me think!"

Her mind was haunted with past failures. Once Murdock had noticed that she always lost a coin toss, the whole phenomenon had become a source of utter embarrassment. And that dang narwhal kept bringing it up, making it worse. Nukilik had started losing sleep over it.

Every time I make a choice, it turns out I'm wrong.

I don't understand! Why? Why does that always happen?

00:59

The countdown clock on the timer descended toward zero.

Top wire?

Or bottom wire?

Nuk hovered her claw over the former, then changed her mind and moved it to the latter.

Nukilik agonized. She'd never made the right call since becoming hyper.

She was paralyzed with indecision.

Wait, she thought, suddenly, hopefully. *That's the key! Since becoming hyper . . . !*

Her run of "bad luck" never used to be a thing.

And she knew exactly why.

"You're overthinking it," she said.

Nukilik glanced at the bomb in its entirety for a split second. Something caught her eye, and she instinctively made up her mind. She swiped at the bottom wire, plucking it free of the battery pack.

The polar bear dared a peek at the countdown clock and let out a final scream.

CHAPTER THIRTY-ONE

ARIEF
(Pongo abelii)

Arief knew so little about what was happening. He was operating off pure instinct. There was no way for him to know how much time they had, but if the turtle's sense of urgency was any indicator, there wasn't much time at all.

He scrambled onto all fours, assessed his surroundings. The factory interior was empty, but a steady stream of stragglers remained on the grounds. Brianna Lennox was one of the last to file out of the atrium. She looked calmer and more collected than most, and lingered where she was in order to help the final kid models find their way to safety.

"Hurry!" Arief shouted at the last of the partygoers. "Get away! Run for cover! There's a bomb in the truck!"

And then a large white form rose from the grass in front of him. With a spasm, it spread its wings and loosed a hellacious cackle. "Ti-i-i-i-ime's up," it taunted at the ape, lifting into the night sky. "This factory's last day of polluting has ari-i-i-i-ived!"

What is THAT thing? Arief shuddered. *A hyper bird?*

But his attention suddenly shifted to something even more alarming and urgent: the sound of a polar bear shrieking.

Arief's gaze whipped toward the truck on its side. He was familiar enough with Nukilik to know she wasn't screaming in fear or pain, but he couldn't figure out what was going on until her cries resolved into . . . laughter.

Victorious laughter.

"I did it!" hollered the bear. Her voice was muffled but plain. "I'm alive! Suck on that, Murdock! I plucked the right wire!"

Arief abandoned the ghostly gull and galloped over

toward the celebratory whoops. "Status update!" he demanded.

Wan popped up from the smashed cavity of the topside driver's door window. "Nukilik disarmed the bomb!" she cheered.

"Is she trapped in there?" Arief asked. "Is she hurt? And where's Murdock? We need to get out of here before we draw any more attention."

"I'm en route!" Murdock blurted over their comms. "I'll be in position for rapid extraction in ninety seconds, over."

Arief could swear that he heard the sound of aircraft propellers in the background of the narwhal's surprising declaration. "Murdock, please tell me you're not somehow piloting *Red Tail*?"

"And yet, somehow, I am," Murdock cheekily replied.

Arief spared exactly one second trying to figure out how that was possible and gave up. "Nukilik, are you safe in there?" he called over to the trapped polar bear.

"I'm hurt, I think. But I'll live. I can't really move. The fumes are bad in here too. Be careful if you come any closer."

"The turtle welded the back door shut," Wangari

explained. "Nuk's wearing a mask, but we still need to get her out fast."

Arief did a quick 360. Most of the humans were beyond the wall and out of sight, for now. But a few of the guards lingered near the gatehouse. At least one of them was watching Arief. He held an excited rottweiler on a taut leash and seemed about ready to release it. "We need to be fast," Arief remarked.

"I've got a plan for the van, orangutan," Murdock trumpeted. "Stand by."

Arief nodded with satisfaction. He had a plan too. He spied Brianna Lennox at the back of the line of stragglers heading out. A guy wearing a silver suit painted to look like a barracuda came running full-tilt out from around a blind corner. He slammed into Brianna from behind. Brianna fell to the ground, hard, with a surprised cry, but the barracuda dude didn't even slow down to help her.

This is my chance, Arief thought. He rushed over to the fallen pop star.

He slowed on his final approach, grew upright, and tried on his warmest smile. "Can I help you up?" he asked her.

Brianna stood slowly, holding back her obvious

frustration. "Just a sec. I need to straighten my leg."

Arief waited while she made an adjustment to her prosthetic limb. "Your bow tie needs straightening too," she told him when she saw him staring.

Arief offered up a chuckle. "I think you're right," he said, fidgeting with the knot.

"Was there really a bomb over there?" she asked, pointing to the truck. "I wasn't going to leave until I knew all the kids were safe."

"I don't know," Arief answered. "But I'm impressed with your principles. Wish I could say the same for everyone else tonight."

"There's been a lot of chaos, no question about that."

Arief nodded knowingly. He cleared his throat. "You still need to get past the wall—just to be safe."

"And who are you again?" Brianna Lennox inquired, giving Arief a hard look.

"I'm just a friend," the orangutan answered. "Listen, I wanted to give you something. It's my only copy, so I'm putting my full trust in you—to do something meaningful with it."

"What is it?" the teen asked, brushing curly red hair from one side of her face.

Arief handed her his head cam. She turned it over in her hand, waiting for an explanation.

"There's a memory card in there with an interesting conversation on it that I want you to see. Don't show it to anybody, though, until after you get home. And then do with it . . . what you feel you need to."

"Okay," Brianna Lennox promised, curious. "But if this is a demo for your monkey-themed band," she joked, "I don't forward that sort of thing along. Just a fair warning."

"It's not," said Arief. "Trust me, you'll want to see this."

Arief could hear the signature thumping of *Red Tail*'s approach, coming in low over the jungle canopy. He gave the pop-star-slash-teen-model a respectful salute and then turned his back to her, mindful to walk upright on his way to the truck.

Arief knew the information contained on that video would never amount to much if he tried to use it himself. Whether or not Scenic Trails ever came to justice for the company's horrible, unethical practices . . . it was in Bri's hands now.

Red Tail came to the scene as the last of the party-goers filtered out. Murdock lowered a thick cable with a metal hook, and Wangari knew right away what to do with it. She attached the end to the back gate of the cargo hold. Murdock piloted the aircraft to the side and up, snapping the sea turtle's hasty welding job. A pile of fifty-five-gallon drums spilled out along with a muddy purple-and-blue polar bear.

"Oh, that's a sight!" Murdock cried over the airwaves with delight. "You look like an Easter egg, Nuk!"

Nuk was in too much pain to even try a comeback. She favored her front left paw heavily and cradled the disarmed bomb like a football. Arief helped her out of the truck and gently took the bomb into his own possession.

"That was a close call," he told her.

She peeled the gas mask from her snout and winked. "Yeah. We *bearly* made it," she said. "Let's get you back to the Ark, to the medical bay as fast as possible," Arief suggested.

He turned to Wan. "Time to make tracks. You better have a lock on that sloth."

The pangolin fished through her vest and came up with a small smartphone. She tapped the glass, gave the display a quick glance, and nodded. "Not surprisingly, he hasn't gotten far."

"Go get him," Arief instructed.

"I'll be back," she said. Then she pointed with her chin toward the guardhouse. "What are you going to do about the guards?"

Arief looked and saw one guard watching the Endangereds from within the safety of his post. One of the rottweilers stood looking out the glass window with him.

Fig shoots, Arief thought, holding his gaze steadily upon the guard as the two contemplated each other.

The orangutan lifted a hand to his mouth and placed his pointer finger in front of his lips. "Shhh!" he warned from across the big lawn, trying very hard not to laugh.

Martín stepped back, standing tall and stiff. He nodded, hesitantly at first, and then more vigorously. Arief shot out his arm, pointing firmly at the forest behind the gatehouse. *We're always watching!*

The guard got the message. He yanked on the dog's chain, and the two of them exited the checkpoint and ran as fast as the human's legs could carry him away from the factory into the dark.

A long moment later, the Endangereds were all on board *Red Tail*, the pigmy three-toed sloth included, and the group set a course for nearby Escudo Island.

Murdock was in his tank, but the tank was dry. "I didn't have time, nor a way, really, to fill it first," he explained through his glass barrier. "I wormed through the swamp to the landing site, made my way up the cargo ramp, and then rerouted controls to my touch displays."

"How'd you see where you were flying, though?" Wan asked, impressed.

"Belly cam and remote sensors."

The sloth clung to Arief's chest, and he gave the grateful creature a pet on the head. "We need to remove this guy's other tracker," he explained to Wan. He positioned the sloth hanging from his neck so that the pangolin could inspect his hairy backside.

Wan gently dislodged the CEO's tracker burred into its greenish fur and used the pliers on her utility knife to destroy it. "Done," she announced.

"They won't harass me anymore?" the three-toed pigmy sloth asked. He looked very relieved.

"No, they won't," Arief promised. "And we'll have

you back in your native habitat shortly."

"Now, let's not be hasty," the animal rebutted. But a delayed wink assured the team that he was attempting a joke. They all laughed together.

It was after the sloth was home again, and *Red Tail* was back in the air heading for the Ark, that Arief dropped his celebratory smile. "I want to know everything about those other two animals," he demanded of the group.

"The brainies?" asked Nuk, rubbing her injured arm. "They're nuts."

"Brainies?" Arief probed.

"We don't know much!" Murdock warned from his tank, freshly filled with warm Atlantic salt water. "But here's what I can tell you. . . ." And he and Nukilik recounted everything they could remember.

"And you triple-checked *Red Tail* this time?" Arief said when they were done. "You're absolutely certain neither of them are stowed on board somewhere?"

"No stowaways," Murdock insisted.

Arief frowned, deep in thought. "I don't like it. First Quag, and now this. It's official: we're not the only hyperintelligent animals operating out there."

During one of their first missions, which had taken the Endangereds to the Four Corners region of the southwestern United States, they had discovered a plot by a demented hyper named Quag, who had harnessed his intellect to somehow build a rudimentary mind-control device that he used to enslave a colony of prairie dogs.

"Are these brainies connected to Quag somehow? Is that critter behind this?" Murdock demanded.

"We need to find out," Wan said.

"We've got enough human-caused fires to put out as it is." Nukilik growled. "We can't expect to run around the globe battling other *animals* now too."

"We may not have much of a choice in the matter." Arief frowned. "There's more going on here than we realize, and I want to get to the bottom of it, fast."

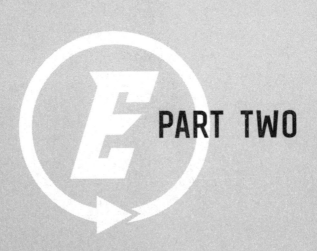

PART TWO

CHAPTER THIRTY-TWO

NUKILIK
(Ursus maritimus)

The Galápagos Islands, Ecuador

After a long flight *Red Tail* touched down before dawn at the Ark. The bay door closed, and the propellers came to rest. The Endangereds filed out of the craft, doing one last check for stowaways at the insistence of Arief, who wasn't taking any chances. Murdock's tank water was drained via a network of hoses into a filtration system. This prevented invasive plants, animals, and insects picked up in Atlantic waters from establishing in the fragile Galápagos ecosystem.

Nukilik was grateful to be able to massage her bruised ribs and battered muscles. More than anything, she was ready for a bath. She had elected not to rinse off while on Escudo Island on account of the damage it might do the sloth's home.

Nukilik limped down the ramp, favoring her broken front paw. She was exempt from helping to refuel and restock *Red Tail*, tasks that always immediately followed landing—no matter how tired the gang was. It was critical that the Endangereds always be ready to launch, with full supplies, at a moment's notice.

She took a seat at the Big Top's computer station with its giant array of flat screen monitors. The Big Top was a part of the Ark which had been entirely forgotten by the humans who had constructed the place. Its original purpose was as a backup chamber designed to relieve pressure inside the rest of the Ark. The primary pressure control chamber on the other side of the island was identical, but it was visited by humans too often. That left this forgotten space as an ideal common area where the animals could gather without having to worry about humans stumbling upon them.

"*Red Tail* never received any tracking alerts while we were out," Arief began, "but review the security footage anyway, will you, Murdock?" The narwhal had just slipped out of the empty aircraft tank and into the saltwater pool at the center of the Big Top. "Nuk, maybe you can do a quick schedule check and track the whereabouts of staff."

Nukilik sighed. As ready for a cleanup as she was, Murdock was right: this couldn't wait. There could be no surprises when it came to the whereabouts of the few humans who ran the island. She typed in the name of Dr. Caitlyn Fellows, as well as her primary assistant, Felix Gooding, into the search bar of the spyware program they used. "No hits since we last left," she reported. "And the poo-bots aren't logging any behavior anomalies for our habs. Looks like no one noticed our absence."

"Great," Arief said while dragging a hose over to *Red Tail*'s fuel tank. "Now head on up to the medical bay and scrub down. And we'll get you fully x-rayed and stitched and bandaged."

"Look at all that blue and purple. You look like a monster from a Pixar movie," chuckled Murdock. "I've got your code name for our next op: Sulley."

As usual, Nukilik had no idea what Murdock was referring to.

"Murdock!" sniped Arief. "Get on the feeds. Review them for anything out of the ordinary while we were gone."

"Aye, aye."

Exhausted but eager to freshen up, Nukilik pushed through the exit hatch. A strong wind blew into the chamber as she shoved it open. It slammed shut behind her. She could feel the pressure building in her ears as she limped up the long corridor to the topside world of the Ark.

Almost all the habitats were under a massive plexiglass dome formed by an interlacing steel framework. A diverse series of biomes were arranged by ecosystem type. Artificial streams and trails ran throughout. Some of the pathways were raised, providing lofty overlooks into the enclosures. Nukilik surfaced through a stairwell disguised as a rock formation near the grassland hab. She climbed a spiral stairway onto the skywalk to the administrative wing of the complex, where the medical bay, vet clinic, and crew quarters were located.

When she had first arrived here, the place had been teeming with construction crews and visitors in business suits, as new habs were being put into place. But now the Ark was back to normal: mostly silent and still. The purple polka-dotted polar bear took her time strolling above her new realm. It wasn't the Great Realm, by any stretch, but it was beginning to feel like home.

CHAPTER THIRTY-THREE

ARIEF
(Pongo abelii)

After several scrub-downs, Nukilik's blondish-white pelt was mostly clean. *The mud is gone, at least*, Arief thought to himself quietly. There were places where the dye colors were still noticeable. But at least Nukilik had no serious chemical burns and was no longer at risk of absorbing toxins. The polar bear was very lucky that she had been so covered in dried muck when she was trapped inside the delivery truck.

"You'll have to try and stay in the shadows when Dr. Fellows visits tomorrow," Arief sighed.

"What if the humans notice the paint job?" Wan asked from atop the counter where she had planted herself.

Arief had no answer for that. The day was going to come when Dr. Fellows figured out that some of the animals at the Ark were more than they seemed. It was Arief's job to delay that moment as long as possible. A polka-dotted polar bear with broken feet and bruised ribs was exactly the sort of thing that could blow their cover.

"I've got an idea," Murdock broadcasted from overhead speakers. His voice echoed like a god figure throughout the entire Ark.

"We're all in one spot, Murdock!"

"Sorry, need to shut off the master volume."

The narwhal audibly fidgeted with the PA system from his sea aquarium, fixing it so that his voice was only piping into the medical bay. "I have a better idea. Let's cover her in flour or baby powder."

"Please, no," Nukilik grumbled.

"Are you kidding?" said Murdock. "Baby powder's luxurious!"

"Better than nothing," Wan seconded.

Arief nodded his agreement too.

Nuk growled but didn't fight the decision.

Arief switched gears. "I've looked at the X-ray imagery. One of the bones in the palm of your paw has a hairline fracture. I don't think it needs to be set. I'll wrap a splint and give you a sling after tomorrow. Keep your weight off it the best you can. It'll heal quickly. Please try not to let Fellows see you limp, or you'll end up getting more attention than you want."

"I can tough it out."

"I still can't believe you survived that tumble inside the truck," Murdock sputtered.

"My mother named me Strength for a reason."

"All right, everyone, you know your tasks." Arief started holding up fingers. "One: put everything in this room back exactly where it belongs. Two: remember to replenish your scat reserves over the next couple days. For every deposit you provide the bots, store one away in your sealed biohazard bags so the Poop-Es can keep collecting during our next away mission. Three: record at least two new hours of natural behavior in your hab so we can loop newer material into the security archive footage. Four, five, and six: everybody, let's get some rest. That's an order."

The team got to work.

The next day started off well. Fellows and Gooding arrived by airplane right on schedule, flying over the dome and taxiing down the island's short runway. Their visit was typical and routine. All throughout the day they moved from hab to hab, running through a checklist on each animal and monitoring the overall health of the plants and trees in all the biomes. Three other staff arrived on the same flight to attend to their own assigned tasks, conducting tests of the facilities. They serviced the Poop-E fleet and jumped on necessary repairs. They replaced filters in each of the air, freshwater, and saltwater circulatory systems. And they topped off the food supplies for the automated meal delivery network.

Arief was feeling good about the visit. He had even received a report from Nukilik that her checkup had gone smoothly, with no obvious suspicion coming from the human caretakers. He was proud of his team, who'd managed to take care of every little detail even though their last mission had turned out to take longer than expected.

Dr. Fellows paid a personal visit to Arief.

"Hi, Pongo!" the vet began when she strolled into

view. Arief's biome was sealed within a glass rectangular cube several stories tall, beneath the dome's apex. It rained within the cube multiple times a day, and the humidity was locked in. The cube was full of lush jungle vegetation and a variety of at-large wildlife, including tropical birds, frogs, insects, and a select number of non-venomous snakes. A stream featuring several kinds of fish looped through the exhibit, fed by a waterfall that rushed down a display of fake rocks. Wangari's cage was next to her own, but she was nowhere obvious right now, probably sleeping in one of her burrows.

Arief had a greeting routine with Dr. Fellows, and he stuck to the script now, in the hopes of speeding up the visit. He approached the links of his enclosure nearest the walking path and gave her a big smile.

"Good to see you too, boy!" Fellows laughed. "Everything going well in here? Anything to report, sir?"

Arief sat down monkey-style, another part of his routine, and looked around expectantly for the apple he knew the vet would produce out of her satchel. *Nothing to see here*, he thought sardonically. *Let's have the ceremonial apple and then time to move along, folks—*

"What happened to you, Pongo?" Dr. Fellows

expressed with sudden concern. "Is that a *burn* on your tummy?"

Arief looked down at his pooching gut, a move which was itself a big no-no; it could indicate to Fellows that he was understanding her too well. *What is she talking about? Oh—no!*

"Is that an electrical burn, sweetie?" Dr. Fellows dropped her satchel and her clipboard and walked around to the side door of the orangutan enclosure. She was coming in.

Arief looked between the vet and his singed stomach in disbelief. He was furious with himself. *How could I have missed this?*

That one-eyed, three-flippered sea turtle was officially on Arief's feces-throwing list.

"Can I come up to you, Pongo?"

Dr. Fellows was respecting Arief's right to personal space, but she wasn't going to take no for an answer. If Arief refused to safely allow her to approach, she'd just tranq him. He indicated with his body language that he was okay with her coming over to inspect his belly. He lowered his gaze and slouched, placing an upward-facing palm on the ground.

Dang. Arief's heart started racing. *This is just going to have to play out now.*

Dr. Fellows took a long look at Arief's burn and his singed hairs. She was close up and concerned, probing the area with her fingers. "How could this have happened, sweetie? It's not a very bad burn, but it's not okay that this happened at all." She unholstered her radio and depressed it. "Felix, come over to Pongo's exhibit. He's burned himself, and we need to figure out how. Priority one."

The vet rose and started turning in a 360 circle, scrutinizing her surroundings. Arief followed her gaze and caught movement near the cable netting shared between his enclosure and Wangari's.

The form scurried off, undetected by Dr. Fellows. But both Arief and Fellows were surprised to find a stock-still Poop-E robot parked in the corner of the enclosure, half-hidden by rain forest undergrowth.

Arief grinned from ear to ear, stifling an outright laugh of relief.

The poo-bot was disabled and positioned with one of its articulating arms out, holding the end of a severed cable that belonged to Wangari's lighting fixtures.

"Huh," said Fellows, talking to Arief. "This bot got snagged somehow on Pinecone's cage wiring! Did you get too close, Pongo? Looks like everything shorted out—at your expense. How terrible!"

Arief raised an arm at the poo-bot and offered up a hiss.

"I figured it out, Felix," the vet reported to her hand-held radio. "Bring a replacement bot to the cube. And some antibacterial ointment. And have one of the guys get down here for a quick electrical job."

"I owe you big," Arief said to the bushes located in the next enclosure over, once all the craziness had run its course.

Wangari crept out of the understory, looking around to make sure the coast was clear. "No problem at all. Glad that worked."

Arief rubbed at the ointment that Dr. Fellows had applied to his zapped belly. "That was really bad," he sighed. "But thanks for having my back."

"We always have each other's backs," Wan reassured him with a wink. "And each other's bellies. But you slipped up . . . because you're exhausted. You need to get some rest. That's an order."

CHAPTER THIRTY-FOUR

WANGARI
(Phataginus tetradactyla)

Late the next day, the team gathered in the Big Top to debrief and begin scouting a new mission. Wangari jumped on the computers to see if there were any animals out there in need of their help.

Wan wasn't on the feeds for more than a minute before something pretty big started taking shape. "Um, Arief? Hey, you better come check this out!" she called over.

"Did you find a hit?" Arief asked. "What's the animal? What part of the world is it?"

"Look!"

Arief took a seat and glanced up at the monitors. The headlines that unfolded before their eyes told quite a story. The articles kept coming:

DEVINE NO LONGER: FASHION ICON FALLS FROM GRACE

SCENIC TRAILS REACHES DEAD END

CONFESSIONS OF CEO POLLUTER SEND SHOCK WAVES THROUGH FASHION INDUSTRY

BRI-LEN BREECHES CONTRACT: DENOUNCES "DISGUSTING" REVELATIONS

CRIMINAL CHARGES CHASE CHAZ

The headlines kept coming. All of them described Chaz Devine and his company in the bleakest of terms. There were references to the extravagant gala and the confusion surrounding a bomb threat, and then there was a separate thread of articles and memes showcasing photo after photo after photo of industry VIPs posing with a highly endangered animal.

There was even a growing debate about the mystery identity of the man in the orangutan suit. The photo of Arief being hugged by the sloth was everywhere.

Wangari looked over at her boss and was a bit startled to catch him blinking away a tear.

"What?" he asked her defensively.

Wangari shook her head, smiling, "Nothing. Nothing at all."

"I knew that teen would come through," the ape said.

"Can you imagine the headlines if those awful brainies had managed to blow that factory up?" She shuddered just thinking about it.

A pop-up message alerted Wan to an incoming video chat request. "Huh?"

She and Arief shared a curious look. Intrigued, Wan swiped away the clutter on the digital desktop and hovered a claw over the Answer Call function.

"Wait," Arief said. "Disable the cam first."

"Good idea." Wan toggled the webcam off and draped a nearby rag over it for good measure. She wasn't sure what to expect. A news reporter somehow tracking the mysterious orangutan-costumed guy down for answers? Brianna Lennox herself? This IP address shouldn't be available to *anyone*. The network protocols only existed here at the Ark, on their remote devices, and on board *Red Tail*, but that—

"Oh, no," Wan grumbled. "I bet I know who's calling."

"Who?" asked Arief.

Wangari growled and accepted the incoming call. A live video feed materialized. "Them," she hissed.

"Sup, broseph!" barked a Pacific green sea turtle wearing a pirate eye patch. He waved a flipper with a prosthetic attachment in greeting. Beside him on the monitor, a giant Laysan albatross coughed.

Wan leaned forward to yank the rag away, but Arief stopped him. "Don't," he whispered. "They might be recording this. Imagine what they could do with footage of us."

Murdock and Nukilik both drew near as the call began. The four Endangereds huddled in a group watching the big screen displays.

"The bird and the turd," growled Nukilik menacingly. "What an unpleasant surprise."

"What do you want?" Arief demanded.

"Better make it good," Murdock added. As he was saying this, he was already busy tracing the origin of the call.

Honu and Mar's background was unrevealing. It was

black, but there was enough texture shining against the surface behind them that she guessed they were looking at a cave wall of some sort.

"We wanted to apologize for any hard feelings," Honu said. "But we need your help with another job."

The Endangereds shared barks of laughter.

"Get real, Honu," said Arief, growing serious.

The computer *ping*ed. Wan glanced up at the wall displays and pointed to make sure Arief saw that Honu and Mar were in . . . Hawaii.

"That's right," Honu said. "Did ya figure out we're on the Big Island? We're home, and we need to pull off a job here. A big one that needs a big ape and big ol' polar bear to make it happen."

"How'd you get hyper?" Arief demanded. "How many of you are there?"

"All in good time, my dear ape. You're not the one with any leverage here, so please do shut up."

Wan couldn't believe what she was hearing. Nobody had a right to speak to Arief that way. "Take that back," Wan growled. "You're delusional if you think you have any say over—"

"Like I told Nukilik, I don't take no for an answer."

Suddenly, the image switched—to a live feed of a bound and muzzled polar bear.

Wan blinked back her disbelief, but the footage was real: a scrawny polar bear lying on its side, all four legs bound together. The bear's eyes were glazed over, and its snout was muzzled. The lack of struggle suggested it was heavily drugged. The animal was on the floor of a cargo hold.

Nukilik leaned in and studied the image more closely. "It's her," she said, her voice gravelly. She suddenly roared her rage and pounded her fists on the desktop. "Let her go! Keep my mother out of this!"

Arief immediately switched off the monitors and muted the connection. He extended a calming hand. "It's a trick, Nuk! Calm down. How can that be her? How can they have her?"

Murdock gurgled. He rose out of the water a little, as if stepping forward. "I think I know how: Mar was with us in the Arctic. He knew where we were. He had plenty of time to snoop around our cockpit and our computers. He could have easily clued into the fact that

Atiqtalik was important to Nuk. The timing is tight, but if they have others in their group, it's not impossible that they really could have kidnapped her."

Wan realized her jaw was gaping and remembered to shut it. "This is a nightmare," she said under her breath.

Arief spoke up, capturing more of the pangolin's own thoughts. "We underestimated them."

"We need to rescue my mom!" Nukilik demanded.

"Agreed. And to do that, I think we have to play along. We won't be missed from the Ark for another week. Our best course of action is to take their offer and go to Hawaii."

"What about my *mom*?" Nukilik insisted.

"She's the mission, Nuk," Arief reassured her. "Absolutely. But she could be captive *anywhere*. Our only chance to track her down is to do what they say and follow the clues."

"Trace this footage," Nukilik demanded of Murdock.

"I am," she explained. "The ping back is the same: Big Island of Hawaii. But I wouldn't draw any conclusions from that. They might just be feeding us a video of a video taken *anywhere*."

Arief unmuted the connection. "Tell us where that bear is."

"There you are!" Honu chimed in. The feed switched back to the brainies. He and Mar were staring at the camera, extremely pleased with themselves. "Are you seeing things our way, or not? Just let me know." Honu smirked. "Mamma Bear could be shipped to the Phoenix Zoo within the week. Or maybe someplace warmer. Riyadh? Dubai? At least she'll be *fed*, poor starving thing. Just saying. Your call."

"And you claim to be for the animals!" Nuk spat. "You disgust me."

"Your mother is safe," the albatross replied. "She's in a refrigerated—"

Honu smacked the bird, and he fell out of sight, groaning and croaking off camera for a moment before struggling back into view.

"We are for the animals," Honu insisted. "But who are *you* for?" He launched into what sounded like a practiced speech. "We represent the greater good. Sacrifices happen along the way. But animals around the world need a champion who can make the hard choices. How many *species* have to go extinct, Arief, before you open your eyes and realize what's truly at stake? The rise of *Homo sapiens* has spelled the doom of biodiversity on Earth. We're in the throes of this planet's sixth great extinction! We're losing as many as a hundred and fifty species a day, Arief! And the humans are spreading, growing, multiplying. Always. Hacking and burning and plowing and bulldozing deeper and deeper into the last wild places, including your precious Arctic, Nukilik. WHEN DOES IT STOP?"

"You sound as wacky as Quag," Wangari scoffed. Even if they deserve it, we won't use violence against the humans."

"Who's Quag?" spat Mar.

"I've heard of him," Honu said dismissively. "He went rogue. He was in it for himself. We're different."

"Well, you're not wrong about one thing," Arief admitted. "The humans are everywhere; they're also part of the life on this planet. We can't kill humans to save other animals—that's not who we are."

"You fools waste your time rushing around the world to rescue individual animals, while there's one easy way to fix the problem for all animals at once—we take power. We demand respect through constant displays of force. We put humans in their place."

"Enough," Arief demanded. "What's the job, Honu?"

Honu considered the question for a minute. Finally, he answered, "We're trying to build a sanctuary— free from tourism and fishing—with tide pools and a secluded beach. We have the perfect place and securing it will help a whole crowd of marine species. Are you happy now? I'll brief you further once we're all together."

"We're in," Arief told Honu. "But this is a one-off. And then you give us Nuk's mom—*unharmed in any way*. Do you hear me? I want that muzzle and those bindings off her *now*. And you have to promise no humans get hurt."

"Yeah, yeah," Honu said, waving off Arief. "No humans will be harmed. Promise."

"Untie her," Nukilik demanded. "I want to see it done."

Honu shook his head. "We'll do it . . . as soon as you send us evidence that you're on your way. We're not stupid."

"We're brainy!" Mar emphasized, finally getting a word in.

Honu knocked him off his seat again. "Meet us at

these coordinates by tomorrow morning."

"We can't be there that fast," Arief was quick to say. "Be reasonable."

Honu tapped his flipper on the desktop in front of him, thinking. "Fine. You have until noon."

The call ended abruptly. A set of coordinates materialized, and the map display automatically zoomed in. A crosshairs appeared on the southern shore of the Big Island of Hawaii, a little to the right of the boundary of Volcanoes National Park, where instructions indicated they seek out the mouth of a lava tube, a sort of tunnel formed after hot lava has quickly drained away underground. Wan assumed this was the entrance to the brainies' headquarters.

"I don't like this," Murdock weighed in. "We're marching into a trap."

"No," Arief insisted. The orangutan cracked his knuckles. His eyes narrowed, and he pounded his chest. "They are."

CHAPTER THIRTY-FIVE

NUKILIK
(Ursus maritimus)

East of Volcanoes National Park, Big Island, Hawai'i

The southern coast of the Big Island of Hawai'i filled the view from Nuk's window in *Red Tail*'s cabin. Sheer black cliffs held back a constant onslaught of powerful ocean waves and breaking sea-foam. Everything about the island seemed dramatic. The ocean was impressively blue, with a dazzling aquamarine ribbon churning all along the deep waters. Past the cliffs, the volcanic terrain took center stage. Layer after layer of ancient lava fields laid one over the next, alternating shades of black and dark brown like a brownie's cake and crust. The forests upslope were thick with native 'ōhi'a trees. Cloud banks blocked Nuk's view of the upper reaches of the volcanic peaks, but even the clouds here were somehow whiter and fluffier than any clouds she could remember.

Nukilik had learned a lot about the Hawaiian archipelago, or island chain, during the flight. Isolated in the middle of the vast Pacific Ocean, the Hawaiian Islands were home to numerous truly unique—and fragile—ecosystems. The Big Island was larger than all the other Hawaiian islands put together. From the cockpit, Nukilik could only see a small portion of what it had to offer, but its charm was already obvious.

The team overshot the jagged coast, circling toward the landing area a half mile inland. The Endangereds had been instructed to touch down inside a wide, deep hole visible in one of the old lava flows. The shadowy shaft blended in with the black terrain and was difficult to spot.

Nukilik finally spied the large hole in the crust, made note of its shape and exact location, and then cleared out of the area, flying directly south to the coastal cliffs.

Arief offered a satisfied nod. "We got here in eight hours, team. Good work. And with a four-hour time difference between here and home, that gives us ample time to scope things out before they start watching for our arrival at noon local time."

Minutes later, *Red Tail* jettisoned Murdock into the ocean and touched down on a secluded slab of old, sea-level lava surrounded by tropical trees. The team filed out and made their way over a stretch of black lava rocks to a cliffside bay. The balmy air had a familiar saltiness, but Hawai'i smelled different than the Galápagos. Nukilik's powerful nose detected more floral scents on the breeze.

The Endangereds huddled together, staring toward a gaping cave opening in the sheer vertical cliff wall.

"This has to be the other end of the lava tube that they want us to meet at," Nukilik surmised.

"I'm counting on it," said Arief. "But let's be sure. Wan, time for you to snap some vacation photos."

"Smile for the camera!" Wan winked and sprang away, smartphone in hand, hopping from one jagged outcropping of black lava rock to the next. If their calculations were correct, Wan would have to trudge a half mile into the tube before coming across the brainies' landing coordinates. Then she'd do some spying, find out any new details she could, and hurry back out.

Murdock breached the surface of the tide pools in front of Nuk and Arief. He'd found a channel that was deep enough to allow him access to the shallows. "Aloha," he spurted. "Come on in, the water's nice. The coral's gorgeous down here. I've already spotted my first humuhumunukunukuapua'a, the Hawaiian state fish!"

"Can you enter the tube?" Arief asked.

Murdock shook his tusk back and forth. "Almost. But not really. There's a small black sand beach developing at the base of the cliffs. I can run aground there, but I can't climb the jagged lip of the cave."

"Map it all out," Arief told Murdock. He glanced at the timepiece he kept on his shoulder belt. "We've got five hours left before we're officially due to arrive. I want everything in place, with an hour to spare."

"Copy that, boss," trumpeted Murdock as he dove beneath the surface and got to work.

Once Wan came back with whatever new information she would find out, Nukilik and Arief would help her set up a series of signal repeaters within the tube, to maintain a strong satellite link at all times. Additionally, on the tube's ceiling and also along the surface, they were going to lay a cable connecting a series of micro detonators to an electronic switchboard under his control.

Arief hoped he wouldn't have to collapse the tube for any reason, but he wanted options in place to foil any escape plans the brainies might have.

"There's a lot of unknowns here," Nukilik confessed. "Are you sure we have the upper paw?"

"We'll learn all we can. We'll be ready for just about anything," Arief assured her. "Speaking of paws, how's your hand feeling?" he asked.

Nukilik waved him off. The truth was, her paw ached a great deal, but she didn't want the team to go easy on her. "Better already. If it hurts it has more to do with this sharp ground than anything!"

"Two kinds of lava here," Arief explained. "A'a, and pahoehoe. Lava can either explode out of volcanic vents, or ooze out of them. Pahoehoe—the smoother, wrinkly-looking stuff we're on now—oozes and cools slowly. A'a is much rougher. It hardens fast while mixing with air. You can't walk on that stuff without cutting yourself to shreds. Luckily, there's usually a way to stick to the glossier stuff."

"I'll deal," Nuk said.

A larger-than-usual wave crashed against the natural breakwater, sending a sky-high blast of salt water and seafoam spraying down upon the two friends. It felt nice on Nukilik's back against the hot morning sun.

"We'll get to the bottom of this, Nuk," Arief said. "Your mother's safety is our number one priority."

Nukilik nodded, but she was hesitant to say anything more. She had a lot on her mind.

As they scrambled over the lava to reach the mouth of the cave, Nukilik noticed railroad tracks leading out of the tube. "What's that?" she asked Arief.

"Huh. Looks like a mine cart line." Arief frowned. "Must be the brainies. They're excavating. The debris they're hauling out of the tube is being turned into that patch of black sand beach." Then he gasped. "Look." Several strange elongated lumps were at rest there, huddled together but obvious. Nukilik instinctively knew what the forms were: seals.

Arief confirmed it. "Hawaiian monk seals. *Neomonachus schauinslandi.*"

Nukilik waited for more, and the ape continued. "I was hoping we'd meet some, though I wasn't holding my breath. They're critically endangered."

They made their way slowly over the difficult terrain toward the cliffside cave. Nukilik was silent, but her troubled thoughts were growing louder.

"They're the only mammals, other than a species of bat, that are native to the Hawaiian Islands," Arief explained. "There're less than fifteen hundred Hawaiian monk seals left. I'm worried about this colony being so close to Honu and Mar's lair. The species is super vulnerable to an extinction vortex. That's when a population gets so small, there's no way for it to grow back. A bad hurricane, or earthquake, or a volcanic eruption can easily wipe out enough of them that the species won't ever recover."

The silence lingered. Big waves collided against the breakwater behind them, and the tidepools, splashed with hints of brilliant colors from below, rippled.

"Whatever unfolds, we've got to keep a close eye on this colony," Arief concluded.

"Copy that," Nukilik said. She couldn't hold back her questions any longer. "What do you think about what Honu said about extinctions? I looked up the numbers he was telling us. A *lot* of species *are* going extinct right now. Are we doing enough good?" She felt guilty just for asking. The ferrets they'd recently gone to great lengths to rescue had been her friends. And they were here to rescue *one* polar bear, her own mother.

Arief stopped, planting both knuckles on a bare patch of wave-worn pahoehoe. He stared out at the vast ocean horizon, took a deep breath, and let it out. "Think about our larger mission this way, Nukilik: we're dealing with the most urgent situations. That's not to say we don't want to save the world. But I think we're wise enough to know that it's not so easy. What we *can* do is save the sloth. And your mother. And maybe these seals . . . and notch bigger wins like taking down Scenic Trails whenever possible. There's good in that, Nukilik. I believe that good begets good. We're depositing coins in a bank. The investment grows into something bigger over the long haul. A lot of individual wins can add up to real change."

Nukilik was new to metaphors and analogies, but she thought she understood what Arief meant: they had a big job to do, but that shouldn't stop them from doing the little things too.

CHAPTER THIRTY-SIX

WANGARI
(Phataginus tetradactyla)

Makai Estates, Big Island, Hawai'i

After several hours of spying, secret planning, and setting booby traps, the Endangereds were back in the air.

Wangari had not found Atiqtalik, Nuk's mother. Nukilik had insisted on another high sweep of the greater area, hoping clues might pop out at them—an odd building or makeshift structure out on the lava fields maybe. Something air-conditioned. The land was dotted with small islands of 'ōhi'a forest, where lava had flowed around a group of trees instead of plowing over them. These "tree islands," called kipuka in Hawaiian, provided habitat for birds and wildlife but not much cover for hiding caged polar bears.

Unfortunately, they weren't finding any evidence of polar bear prisons.

There was a town called Makai Estates on the coast to the east of the lava tube. Wan estimated that it contained around twenty thousand people. *They could be hiding Atiqtalik there somewhere*, Wan thought hopelessly. A quick flyover wouldn't help their search if the polar bear was being held indoors within town limits.

"I'm surprised people live this close to active lava flows," Nukilik shared.

Arief shook his head sympathetically. "Industrial fishing operations and the tourism industry took over this district, among other big changes. Land is cheap where the risks for volcanic activity and air-quality issues are highest. Sometimes these are the only places left where many people can afford to live."

"I'm engaging the landing sequence," Nukilik announced, disappointed in their survey results. She banked suddenly west while steering one-handed. While her broken paw rested in her lap, her uninjured paw left the wheel to flip the switches. Wan suspected the polar bear was in more pain than she wanted to admit. "Make sure I don't eat those two critters the second we see them."

"I'm not sure we could stop you," Murdock worried from his freshly filled tank.

"We'll find her, Nuk!" Wan replied. "Hang in there. We just need some time."

"We're out of time for sightseeing, though," said Nukilik. "The next flock of tour copters will be coming through here any minute."

Helicopter tours left from Makai Estates frequently, as lava was currently flowing over the black landscape inside the boundary of Volcanoes National Park. There were news reports that the flow would reach the ocean's edge any day now, delighting tourists with dramatic views of sea waves crashing into the fiery rock. The plumes of corrosive lava haze, aka laze—a deadly combo of water vapor, chlorine gas, and minuscule shards of volcanic glass—were a sight to behold from above. Unfortunately for local residents, the gases could be bad for their health on windy days.

Arief played back Wan's video surveillance on his

dash display. "Tell me about the layout of the landing spot again."

Wan had spent more than an hour inside the lava tube and had come across the brainies' equipment stashes in multiple places, including the large cavern with the hole in the roof where they were supposed to touch down. "There's plenty of room to land," she reassured him. "The shaft is deep, but it widens out toward the bottom. The lava tube runs like a sideways hose on either side of the landing shaft. One direction lets out to the sea, where we just were, and I have no idea how far upslope the tube continues in the other direction."

"The known record length for a continuous lava tube on the Big Island is about thirty-seven miles," Murdock interjected. "They could have quite an operation down there."

"I don't know about that," Wan said. "As far as I can tell, it's just the two of them. I only ever tracked one pair of flippers and one set of webbed prints. I think Honu and Mar really do need our help to pull off whatever they're working on. That said, as far as hideouts go, it's a pretty sweet setup."

"Did you see what they're using the mine cart for?"

Wan shook her head. "No. But I assume they're hauling crumbled rock from newly drilled tunnels. I only saw that the railway is continuous from the tube mouth at the sea, all the way to here, and then it runs off into darkness."

"I'm certain Honu was lying about their mission objective. But what *are* they up to?" Arief wondered. "I really can't make heads or tails of it."

"That's because you don't have a tail. There's a zoo in Hilo," Murdock speculated. "Maybe they're orchestrating a prison break."

Arief shook his head. "To be honest: if whatever they have planned was that reasonable, I'd be relieved. These guys are thinking bigger—and weirder. I just know it."

Nukilik lined up *Red Tail* and toggled on the autopilot for a guided descent. She double-checked the radar and made a visual confirmation that no tourist helicopters were around to see what they were up to, and the craft descended steadily down a narrow shaft in the volcanic earth.

CHAPTER THIRTY-SEVEN

ARIEF
(Pongo abelii)

The aircraft dropped below ground level and the auto-guidance system faltered with the change in pressure. *Red Tail* pitched forward suddenly. Arief's heart caught in his throat. *We're going to clip the wall!*

But Nukilik was already taking control with her good front paw. She pulled back, correcting for the pressure shift on instinct. The aircraft found its balance and grew steady. She stayed with it, landing manually upon the lava tube floor.

"Nice flying," Arief praised her, combing a hand

through the hair on his head. "That was close."

"I've heard of crashing a party," Murdock said. "That's not what I had in mind, though. Good work."

Nukilik smiled and offered herself a mental pat on the shoulder.

Arief unbuckled his harness and sprang to his feet. Through the cabin windows he saw Honu and Mar approaching out of the darkness upslope. The cavern was lit only by the natural daylight beaming down through the shaft. The sea turtle and the albatross both wore headlamps over their foreheads. Honu's one bad eye was patched, and his multipurpose flipper featured a tool Arief couldn't identify.

Mar held out three flower leis draped over a wing as he awkwardly waddled forward.

"Sup, brosephs!" shouted the turtle over the noise of the slowing tilt-rotor propellers.

"What's a broseph, anyway?" Wangari asked the team, unimpressed.

"It's a dude that's your friend," answered Murdock.

"Oh," said Nukilik in all seriousness. "I thought it was a Joseph that's your brother."

"All right, Endangereds," Arief interrupted. "We're

live. You know the game plan. But stay sharp."

He caught a wink from Murdock, who was frantically tapping on his tank's touch screen display, getting in a few final command protocols before turning off his screen for the time being. "We're linked with the repeaters!" he announced. "Easy peasy. Decryption still in progress—it may take a while, unfortunately. They've got an airtight network set up, I'll give them that. I'll do status checks and nudge things along if I can."

The ramp opened. Arief stepped out first. He immediately noted the cool humidity inside the lava tube and enjoyed the feel of it on his hairy skin.

"Aloha," Honu announced with a flourish, lifting his good front flipper in greeting. "Welcome to paradise!"

"Come get your lei," added Mar. He held out the first of the traditional Hawaiian flower necklaces for Arief. "Don't worry. Made with real plumeria flowers and biodegradable strings."

"Hey, no fair. I want one!" complained Murdock, his voice carrying through the open door.

"We're not on vacation," Arief growled. "Get that out of my face." He shooed the giant albatross away.

"Where's my mother?" demanded Nukilik, hopping off the ramp and storming ahead of Arief toward the sea turtle.

Honu backed away out of instinct but then held his ground. "Take it easy. She's safe. But we've also made arrangements: if either of us can't check in with Mamma Bear's handlers at specified times . . . she'll be shipped to a zoo."

Nukilik lunged forward anyway, and Arief wondered for a split second if she was going to whack the turtle's head down into his shell despite the consequences. But the polar bear kept her cool.

"Are you guys going to allow me out of here?" Murdock demanded.

"You stay in there," ordered Mar. "That was the deal. We get to keep tabs on all four of . . . of . . . *achYOU.*" He sneezed and dropped one of the leis.

"I can't stay in this stagnant tank the whole time we're here. Why'd I even come?" the narwhal complained. "Come on, I'll be swimming in my own pee."

"You should have gone before leaving the house!" scolded Mar.

Arief stood by as Murdock insisted he needed to be

let out. All part of the ruse. It was best if the brainies believed Murdock was genuinely miserable.

"That's enough!" Honu demanded. "You'll have your turn, Murdock. Just wait. We've got a mission to pull off. Follow me! Leave your radios and head cams behind. No secret conversations."

Arief, Wan, and Nukilik each showily tossed headsets back into the cockpit.

Honu turned his head and shone his lamp upslope into the dark. The passage narrowed, but it remained tall enough that Nuk would have no problem walking upright. The walls of the lava tube were visibly smooth like polished black concrete. The ground was flat but rough. The parallel mine cart tracks ran straight down the middle of the tube and perfectly matched the gentle bend in the corridor up ahead.

Arief gave Nuk and Wan a nod of reassurance as they followed the turtle. It was Mar who lagged behind. "Seriously? I went through a lot of trouble for these. No one wants a lei?"

The albatross sighed and ditched the welcome gifts and hurried to catch up with the group, leaving

Murdock, by all appearances, trapped in his tank with nothing to do.

But sometimes appearances are meant to be deceiving.

"What is the mission, Honu?" Arief pressed.

"I'm getting to that," snapped the turtle. "It's easier to show you."

Arief bared his teeth in frustration.

They advanced half a mile into the tube, which turned left and right, and ascended and descended in sections. Occasionally, branching tunnels appeared, some of them stacked above the main line and unreachable without climbing equipment. The floor was rough on Arief's feet and knuckles; it was as painful as walking on gravel. Nukilik continued to favor her injured paw, but it wasn't too noticeable because they were all stepping carefully.

The tube expanded in diameter in some places, becoming quite cavernous, and it shrank enough in others that Nukilik found it hard to stoop through the squeezes. Sometimes they entered areas where long brown roots hung down from the ceiling, soaking up moisture in the air and glistening with dew against the headlamps.

"We're going beneath a kipuka, or forest patch, in the lava field up on the surface," informed their reptilian tour guide. "These are 'ōhi'a roots."

They came to a new passage that looked nothing like the primary lava tube: an artificial corridor. The track swerved into this smaller, more uniform hallway. Honu stopped here and flipped on a light switch. The tunnel lit up, revealing a workbench with strewn tools, a gas generator, and a large, locked toolbox. Discarded in the main corridor was a broken coring machine with a triad of large drill bits. It was supposed to roll on the tracks, but it lay toppled beside them.

"Nukilik," Honu instructed, pointing with his artificial appendage. "Grab that pneumatic rock drill and a jug of airline lubricator. Arief, take up that variable-speed rotary hammer. Mar will show you what to do. Wan, you're with me."

"Finally," said Mar, "we've got someone large enough to operate the jackhammers!"

Mar lifted a wing, indicating to Nukilik to pick up a huge power tool with a massive iron drill bit. Arief noticed a bunch of empty canisters laid on the workbench past the jackhammers. Beyond the canisters: stacked circuit boards and coiled wires. Altogether, the components reminded Arief of the bomb from Panama.

Arief put his knuckles down. "Honu, start talking! What do you need us for? What's the job here? How long do you expect us to be here? Why are there more bombs?"

Honu rolled his eye. "Isn't it obvious by now? We need you big guys to help us move heavy equipment around. Only you can use the manual tools as we get into tighter passages. The industrial drill machine we've been using is kaput, so it's up to you and the jackhammers from here on out. Wan's going to help with our bomb building."

"You said no one would be hurt," Arief growled. He stood tall and balled his palms into fists.

"Simmer down, simian. I know what we said," Honu scoffed. "The explosives are for tunneling."

The Endangereds shared a wary glance but held their tongues. Arief wasn't swallowing any of this. All this work . . . it was a convenient ruse. He wondered if Honu was simply buying time for something bigger.

The irony that the Endangereds were playing along only to buy time themselves was not lost on Arief. He sensed a dangerous game of chicken was afoot.

"But what are the tunnels for, Honu?" Arief insisted. "What are you really up to?"

He suddenly had a strange feeling in his gut. It was a sensation he'd had before. And then he remembered when he had experienced it: As a child, in the moments before an earthquake shook his Sumatran forest. He'd felt the exact same ultra-low-frequency waves vibrating his chest and skull.

"And there's your answer!" Honu crowed. "How's that for dramatic timing!"

Arief wasn't amused. "You're not answering any—"

It happened again. This time it swelled into an actual vibration, accompanied by an audible rumble. A tremor rocked the lava tube. No rocks or debris broke from the walls, but the ʻōhiʻa roots swayed. Arief felt the power of the earth knock against his legs. The tools and the canisters on the workbench rattled. It lasted all of ten seconds and abruptly stopped.

The Endangereds looked around nervously. "I knew it before it happened," Nukilik explained. "Earthquake."

"Relaa-a-a-ax! That was a two point five *at best*," Mar told everyone. "We're above an active hot spot with a bunch of active vents. What do you expect? Tremors happen every day. Get used to it. In fact, this is precisely what you're here to help us with."

"What do you mean?" demanded Wan when the bird paused for too long. "What do you have planned?"

Honu beat the albatross to the punch. "It's simple," he said, pausing for effect. "We're here to jump-start the magma plume and redirect the lava already flowing west of here to cross this way instead—in order to bury Makai Estates."

CHAPTER THIRTY-EIGHT

NUKILIK
(Ursus maritimus)

Nukilik wasn't sure she had heard the sea turtle correctly. Or if she had, she was certain she was missing something. It seemed to her that what Mar was talking about would hurt or kill hundreds, maybe thousands, of people.

"You can't do that," Arief said.

"Wait. Really? We can't?" Mar asked, genuinely shocked.

"Mar! Shut up, you birdbrain!" The sea turtle pointed his bionic flipper at the confused albatross and launched a net at him. The projectile fired with a *pop* and spread open, instantly enveloping Mar.

Honu laughed playfully. "I've been meaning to try that out. Works almost too well."

"Honu, seriously," Arief continued. "Is that really your plan? You're going to destroy the human town using lava? It's the craziest thing I've ever heard."

"That's the plan," Honu said defiantly.

"You can't control nature like that," the orangutan pointed out.

"We're not trying to force an eruption, just to point one in the right direction when it happens. The lava's already flowing along the park boundary, and we know the source magma chamber is close—you'll feel the temperature rise as you get farther down this hall. All we're doing is puncturing through to the existing swell. The flow will find its way into Makai Estates because the terrain tilts that way. Makai Estates is already in a stage-one 'readiness alert,' so the humans should have time to evacuate. If not—well, that's on them."

Nukilik looked to Arief and watched his expression closely. Arief was clearly worried. But was it even possible to intentionally direct a volcanic eruption toward the town? They had to assume the ambitious turtle knew what he was doing.

"But why?" Nukilik asked Honu. "Why would you even want this?"

"Hey. Let me out of here," Mar half asked, half demanded. He was losing patience within the netting.

"You'll figure it out!" shouted Honu. "And then reload my launcher when you're free."

Mar croaked his disappointment but started squirming. A cloud of feathers fluttered up as he loosened the webbing.

Honu turned to Nukilik. "Because without the humans, the whole coast would become national park land. The local coral reef ecosystems would finally be protected. There's a population of monk seals on the beach near Makai. They'd have their privacy back. The fishing industry around here would have to close down. Do you know how hard it is out there for my sea turtle brothers and sisters?"

"Dude," Mar spat at his partner angrily, clearly making progress against the bindings. "You're monologuing!" Wan had walked over to Mar and helped the bird free itself. Nukilik watched closely—she was cutting the netting in places and not just untangling the weights and the lead line. Nuk held back a smirk as she watched the pangolin sabotage the turtle's weapon.

Honu ignored them as he ranted on. "Have you heard the term bycatch? It's when animals get caught in nets by accident; it happens to countless turtles every year, and it's how I lost this." He held up his damaged flipper. "Or think about all the beaches that have been destroyed, beaches that used to be where we would lay our eggs, or all the boats that run us over, or the pollution that chokes our homes. . . . We're facing dangers where we feed, where we nest, and where we sleep. It's a small wonder that there are any of us left at all. Need I go on?"

Wan stood back from the albatross. A second later, Mar freed himself from the sea turtle's net as if he'd just completed an impressive magic act onstage. He held his neck stiff in the air for a beat before hacking something up. It took a remarkably long time to fully emerge. It was a plastic restaurant straw.

"Don't you see? It's up to us. It's time we took back what's ours!" cried Honu angrily.

"No!" Arief beat his chest and slammed his knuckles

down. "We're not here to hurt anyone. We're here to help us all coexist!"

Nukilik lowered her gaze. She wondered if Honu was right. Even if his tactics went too far, maybe the Endangereds weren't going far enough?

"Honu, how can you even be sure this is going to work?" Wan asked as she handed the sabotaged game net back to him. "You're just as likely to harm the monk seals as you are to chase the humans off."

Honu laughed shortly. "This may sound ripe coming from me, but if you want to make an omelet, you've gotta break some eggs."

Arief forgot his calm. He knuckled forward menacingly. "If you start a war now, the animals will be the ones who lose."

"Lose what? What do we have to lose, Arief?"

Nukilik waited for the great ape's response. But the two enemies only stared each other down.

"Enough talk," suggested Mar. "Time for all of us to get to wo-o-o-o-ork."

This got Honu's attention. "You're right for once." He turned to the Endangereds. "Remember the deal about Nuk's mom and focus. Grab your drills. We'll show you where to go."

Honu and Mar led the way down the dead-end tunnel, and the Endangereds followed a few steps behind. The temperature rose noticeably as they advanced, and for the first time the brainies' crazy scheme started to feel scarily real.

"We can't let them destroy a human town," Arief growled to his team.

"No," agreed Wan. "We're getting in deep on this one, though."

"Tell me about it," Nukilik said, touching the wall of the corridor and expecting it to be too hot to touch. It wasn't, but it was warmer than before.

Arief and Wan both looked to Nuk, their shadows lit only by the dim reach of the main corridor lighting. "We have to stop them, no matter what else happens."

Nukilik hesitated but nodded. "Yes. Of course."

"We need to figure out Atiqtalik's location fast," Arief insisted.

Nukilik stiffened.

"Activate the tiny radio fastened deep in your ear,

Wan," said Arief. "Update Murdock. We need that location! And we need readouts for this whole tunnel system. Any drilling we do has to be according to *our* designs."

"I like what I'm hearing." Wangari grinned.

"Great," Arief agreed. "Now let's dig up some dirt."

CHAPTER THIRTY-NINE

MURDOCK
(Monodon monoceros)

Brainy Lair, Lava Tube, Big Island
Three days later . . .

Over the course of several days, Murdock logged countless hours on *Red Tail*'s mainframe—but his progress was sporadic. He could only work on his touch screens when the brainies weren't watching, and unfortunately, Honu or Mar were in the landing chamber *a lot* to tinker with their computers and bomb components.

Infiltrating the host network was proving next to impossible because he had so little time to work. But Murdock wasn't giving up. Atiqtalik's life—and their own lives—and the lives of humans in Makai Estates—were on the line.

Honu and Mar never rested at the same time. They kept Arief, Nuk, and Wan in large animal cages when they weren't working. If Wan could've gotten away for five minutes, the narwhal could've pried open the brainies' computers and hardwired a backdoor interface. But no such luck.

Murdock would have to accomplish the virtual break-in on his own.

The narwhal was proud of his earliest win, at least. Within hours of landing, he had hacked the government-issued lidar processing system that the brainies were using to map the lava tube. Murdock had reoriented the device's digital compass bearings, causing all the maps to show phony data. The brainies were none the wiser, and for the past three days, they had been instructing the Endangereds to dig bogus tunnels.

Day after day, mine cart after mine cart had rolled past Murdock toward the ocean, each one filled with crumbled lava rock hollowed out from the wrong directions.

Murdock had studied the original data before

altering the maps. He'd taken special note: the lava plume responsible for the current surface flow was edging up against the tunnels Honu had been carving. The brainy sea turtle was too brainy for his own good; he had definitely been onto something. If one of the frequent tremors became a slightly larger earthquake instead, the magma pocket might break without the need of anyone's assistance.

In other words, like it or not, the clock was ticking.

But the urgency was growing from all sides. Murdock's water was genuinely filthy at this point, and if the Endangereds weren't back at the Ark by the end of the week, Dr. Fellows would surely notice.

The narwhal got back to work, running algorithms and searching for wormholes in the brainies' server access nodes late into the night.

Early the next morning, Murdock finally made the key discovery he'd been desperate to hack.

A sequence of letters and numbers—a data "fingerprint" so to speak—caught his attention:

CYBORGAKUPARA

"Wait a sec." Murdock let loose a bubble of laughter and leaned in close to his glass display to confirm. "Akupara" was the name of the mythical tortoise in human Hinduism—the tortoise that held the world on its back.

If he's using these terms in passwords . . . Murdock hoped, *then my algorithms can focus on similar patterns.* The narwhal typed the series of symbols into his decryption sequencer and the software began its scan. Within seconds, the system password for the brainies' mainframe surfaced.

Thirty seconds later, Murdock had remotely hacked Honu's computer desktop.

"Great Northern Star," Murdock sputtered. "I'm in!"

It wasn't yet light out, but the crack of sky showing down through the shaft above *Red Tail* had a purple glow. The others were exhausted from work, so he resisted the urge to alert them just yet.

"Okay," Murdock said to himself, "let's take a quick swim around the digital pool and see what kind of info we can churn up."

His first priority was to determine Atiqtalik's location. He began snooping around and quickly started feeling like a beluga in a shrimp factory. *So much to snack on!* he thought delightedly. "What do we have here? Should be interesting." He clicked on a desktop folder with the intriguing label of:

R.A.B.I.D.

The window that opened proved very interesting indeed.

"Radical Animals with Brainy Intellect Directive," he read aloud. "Hmm," he said tastily. "That's a mouthful. Someone really wanted to spell out 'rabid,' didn't they!"

He scanned the folder and noticed it contained a number of subfolders including a firewalled membership manifest. There were other locked subfolders created by Honu, including one labeled "Neuroflexicin supply sched," one mysteriously titled, "Big K oppo-research," and a more chilling archive named "ABC: Arief Borneo Classifieds."

There was one unprotected file at the bottom. *Looks like Honu saved himself a local copy of an outgoing email.* Murdock was giddy. *Must be important.*

He opened it and read the string of back-and-forth communication. The email chain started two weeks ago. The most recent two were from today.

This better be a joke, Honu. You were explicitly told NOT to engage them. They're PLAYING you, idiot. If you muck this up, consider yourself extinct.

—MML

"Your Monitor is watching you back."

Munson baby!

Quick update. Don't want to spoil the surprise, but things are on schedule here. Keep an eye on the *news*. And I've got a bonus catch for you. Let me know how the big Kahuna prefers his Endangereds cooked. ☺

Fine, Honu, but our patience is wearing thin. Costs don't matter but we're unhappy with your lack of deliverables. K expects a real win or you're out. You and that sick bird have one month.

—MML

"Your Monitor is watching you back."

Aloha Munson,

Don't cut off our N-flex yet! You're not wrong about Mar but I'm handling him just fine for the time being. Please send word up the chain: we've got something EXPLOSIVE in the works. I know you can spare the doses. I just need six weeks, and we'll show you just what the boss's investment can amount to.

Murdock grinned. "Well, this is a lot to digest."

He reread one line in particular. *Let me know how the big Kahuna prefers his Endangereds cooked.*

He growled, releasing a rising curtain of tiny air bubbles. *These jerks are planning to do us in!*

That said, there was a treasure trove of information here. Murdock needed to download everything so he and the team could review it all together later.

But he realized that if clues leading to Atiqtalik were stored in any of these locked subfolders, he needed to hack them *now*. He backed out of the R.A.B.I.D. directory and returned his attention to Nuk's mom.

He navigated to the server's internet protocol archives and scanned for live video patches with timestamps.

"Thar she blows," Murdock exclaimed a few seconds

later. He clicked on a raw video clip and found Atiqtalik sleeping restlessly in the corner of a steel hold.

Now I just need to interpret the geopositioning data embedded in the file permissions. . . .

A light flared somewhere outside of *Red Tail*, illuminating the chamber walls of the lava tube.

"Salmon cakes," the narwhal cursed. It was Honu. He had clearly noticed a glowing light coming from inside the craft.

"That you, Murdock?" Honu asked, yawning and rubbing his one good eye with his one good front limb. "What's that light doing on?"

"Uh . . . ," stalled Murdock as he tried to memorize the string of numbers he had just drudged up. He needed more time! But if Honu popped his head into the cockpit, Murdock's secret computer interface inside of his tank wouldn't be so secret anymore. "I'm farming photosynthetic algae!" he shouted angrily, knowing already the explanation was a complete fail. He doubled down anyway. "You're starving me in here. I need *something* to eat!"

"Algae? Seriously, what's the deal in there?"

The coordinates indicate somewhere nearby, Murdock

realized. *Atiqtalik is in Hawai'i!* He quickly focused on memorizing the final few digits of the GPS coordinates, to look them up later. But then his eye snagged on a file listed in a neighboring folder. He clicked it open, praying that he wasn't wasting what little time he had.

That's it! he thought.

He'd found a receipt for a local rental of a refrigerated cargo container.

There was a handwritten note attached to the invoice indicating the container had been parked near an abandoned airport landing strip a few miles north of Makai Estates.

Murdock scrambled to shut off his glowing displays before Honu caught on that they were the source of the cabin lights. Unfortunately, the sea turtle came up the ramp before a full system shutdown was complete.

"You have a computer in the tank?" Honu asked. His good eye narrowed with the realization that this could spell trouble.

"I'm an addict," Murdock pouted. "I'm level eighty on Jewel Crusher, Samurai Class. Don't take away my game!" he begged. "My ranking will plummet! I'll lose my badges!"

"You've had access to *Red Tail*'s onboard computers this whole time?" Honu shouted.

"Cut me some slack. I've got nothing else to do in here. It's not like I can access the global satellite grid from the bottom of this hole." That was a bold-faced lie, given the repeaters they'd established throughout the lower portion of the lava tube and up on the surface, but it was a valiant bluff. "I'm just playing games to keep my sanity intact."

"This is an outrageous breach of trust," Honu snapped. "You're playing *me*! Were you trying to hack my servers? What have you been up to?"

"Honu," Murdock blubbered insistently. "I haven't hacked anything. Come on, turtle! I don't sleep. I've gotta breathe every twenty minutes or I die. I need things to do to pass the time."

Honu stepped inside *Red Tail* and rotated his gadget appendage to his electric welder setting. He let the blue arc crackle for a moment for effect and then thrust his prosthesis at the metal flooring next to Murdock's translucent screens. The surge fried the narwhal's touch screens.

"Noooooooo!" blubbered Murdock. He hadn't yet had the chance to download the R.A.B.I.D. file directory and all the information stored in its subdirectories. He wouldn't get another opportunity to do that now.

"Shut up!" the sea turtle demanded. The cavern grew quiet, and Honu turned in a circle on the open ramp to survey the chamber. He clicked on a radio speaker clipped to his harness. "I know you're up to something. Whatever it is stops now," he announced, waking the rest of the Endangereds, who were caged upslope, "or Nuk's mom will meet her doom. Time is short. Embrace the moment. Can you feel it? You're a part of something spectacular whether you like it or not."

Oddly, Murdock *could* feel it. A new tide of low-frequency waves tickled his rib cage. *Another tremor's coming*, he sensed.

The tremors arrived. The lava tube shook, and Honu's computer rattled off the table and broke on the floor. Murdock's water sloshed. And then all was still again. Honu pressed a button, opening the cages in the darkness of the tube ahead. A moment later, the rest of the team appeared, groggy and annoyed.

"See what I mean?" Honu bellowed. "Nature's on our side! Wake up! We're getting to work early," he told everyone. "Today we unleash the plume!"

CHAPTER FORTY

ARIEF
(Pongo abelii)

Arief listened to the sea turtle's rally cry and balled his fists. He was fed up.

He'd wanted to act late yesterday afternoon, after another tremor, which had lasted almost a minute. But he'd held off. They hadn't located Atiqtalik yet, and he worried that Nuk's focus would be compromised without knowing his mother was safe.

But the situation was getting out of paw. He couldn't stall any longer.

The albatross swooped into view. He landed hard

and stumbled forward. He panted, "Honu, go up top. You've gotta see this!"

"What is it, Mar?" the sea turtle demanded.

"The Pu'u O'o vent . . . it's opened. It's fountaining!"

"What?" Honu snapped excitedly. "You better not be yanking my tail."

"Come see, quick!"

Mar was already taking off, but Honu stopped him. "Wait. I'll go. You escort our guests topside. I want the stupid ape to see this. I want them all to see this. Have them haul a satchel of bombs each, and you bring one too."

The sea turtle marched as he barked orders. He lifted his utility appendage and shot a grappling hook up the shaft. Honu pressed a button, and he reeled out of view above.

"You guys come with me," Mar ordered.

Wangari gave Arief a questioning look, but he shook his head. *Wait.*

It was definitely time to make a move, but . . . Murdock seemed desperate to communicate something. He needed a clearer picture of what was happening before he launched the Endangereds into action.

"You wanna ruffle my feathers?" warned the albatross. He belched for good measure.

Nukilik growled. The albatross gave her a hiss. "You heard the turtle. Climb!"

The polar bear led the way with a snarl of protest. Nuk stormed up the passage toward the surface access ladder. It mounted up through a smaller natural crack in the lava tube's high ceiling. "Grab a satchel!" Mar called after her, but Nukilik ignored the instruction.

Arief frowned. The polar bear was obviously frantic. *She must know that time's almost up*, he figured.

"Get your polar bear's head on straight," Mar warned, flapping his wings at Arief. "She needs to follow orders or her mom will spend the rest of her life eating soggy fish sticks at a dirty zoo."

"Don't worry about Nukilik," Arief hissed. "You watch your own back."

Wan and Arief made tracks toward the ladder, shouldering a bag of bombs each. Mar flew on top of *Red Tail* to keep an eye on them.

"Arief! I need to talk to you," Murdock insisted from his tank.

"You stay put, blubber brain," Mar shouted down at

him. "The rest of you, move out. The clock is ticking."

Murdock swiped his long tusk up and out of the water of his tank, racking the tip against the glass skylight of the cabin, startling the bird above. Mar flapped his wings and took flight, rising up through a shaft of faint but gathering light.

Arief saw the urgency in Murdock's expression, but he kept knuckling toward the upslope ladder. *He'll just have to radio Wan*, Arief decided. *I need to catch up to Nukilik now—before she does something she might regret.*

Arief and Wangari reached the ladder and climbed. Arief's bomb bag was larger, but he easily overtook the pangolin.

"Murdock is onto something. Can you radio him?" the orangutan asked.

"I doubt it. His screens were fried," Wangari answered.

Arief huffed with frustration. "Okay. Go back and find out what he needed to say. But make it quick."

Wan nodded, already sliding back down the length of the ladder. "I'll grab my utility harness while I'm at it," she shouted up.

"Grab mine too, if you can."

Arief raced ahead, clambering out of a hole in the

lava tube and onto the surface, slightly out of breath.

The view stole the rest of his breath away.

About a mile upslope across the darkened lava field, a fountain of fire gushed up through a rent in the Earth's crust. Glowing red liquid spat into the air, flying wide against the purple twilit sky. Lava had gathered into a giant, pulsing orange-black blob that had begun flowing down over the uneven blacktop.

The dark shards of the blob's advancing front were rimmed with glowing, stretching fractures of inner yellow-orange light. The flow spread in all downhill directions, seeking low ground and a path forward. Arief wasn't in any danger, but he could tell its arrival was inevitable.

High above the fountain, Arief could see the looming mass of Mauna Loa silhouetted against the stars. This was his first glance of the ancient volcano. Its higher reaches had been shrouded in clouds when they had arrived.

Mauna Loa meant "long mountain," and it was so named because it looked more like a pitcher's mound than a dramatic, cone-shaped volcano. Arief knew, though, that its size was deceptive. Measured from the sea floor, Mauna Loa was actually taller than Mount Everest.

"Last chance, Honu. Tell me where to find my mother!"

Arief's attention immediately refocused on Nukilik. She was twenty feet away, silhouetted against the spitting fire. She had Honu in her paws, his flippers pinned at his sides.

"She's the only leverage I have, frost breath!" Honu screamed defiantly. "If I tell you anything, I'm dead anyway, aren't I?"

"She doesn't deserve to be your pawn!" the polar bear roared.

"Nukilik, wait!" shouted Arief, galloping closer.

Mar flapped to the ground just out of Nukilik's reach. He set his bag of explosives down, looking everywhere at once.

"Mar! Go!" Honu cried. "Divert the flow toward town! Set the first charges in the tunnels and detonate them!"

The albatross obeyed in a flash, his bombs carried away in his beak.

Nukilik threw down the turtle with a grunt of loathing and lunged for the bird, swiping and missing.

Nuk would have batted him down easily if she had full strength in her broken paw. The albatross soared clear of the attack and dove out of sight into the shaft.

Wangari sprinted to a halt beside Arief. "Murdock found her, Nukilik. Your mother's a few miles away, near the old Makai Estates airstrip." She handed Arief his loaded utility strap.

Arief turned to Nukilik as he swung an arm through his bandolier. The polar bear was taking in the news with a gathering swirl of different facial expressions. "Are you sure?" she asked.

"Positive," she said.

"There's no time to lose," Arief said. "Stop Mar, and then let's go!"

"This is mutiny!" Honu swore over the distant roar of the lava fountain. He backed away a few steps.

A sudden explosion sent smoke and debris skyward. An accompanying jolt in the ground rattled the orangutan's feet. When the dust settled, Arief saw that the lava had found a sudden hole in the earth to pour down through. A bright orange lavafall gushed into the void.

"No." Arief was gobsmacked. Mar had done it. He'd detonated bombs underground. The lava was now channeling toward town.

But Arief held his worry in check. Their work over the past three days, to sabotage and misdirect the planned path of the flow, still stood in the way of Makai Estates' doom.

Wan clicked on her earpiece. "Mayday! Mayday! Murdock! The plume is breached. Lava pouring down below!"

No answer.

"His radio's out." The pangolin barked curses.

"Grab the turtle and get down to *Red Tail*," Arief instructed.

Nukilik lunged forward to apprehend Honu, but he shot her twice, rapid fire, with tranquilizer darts from his flipper. The polar bear keeled over, clutching her gut.

Enraged, Wan rushed forward, but Honu activated a different flipper extension and launched netting at her.

The webbing smashed against Wangari, tangling her up and sending her tumbling backward.

Arief snarled and sprang at the sea turtle himself.

But Honu had already spun his flipper back to its tranquilizer setting.

In midleap, Arief felt a sharp prick at his shoulder, and by the time he hit the ground, he was hardly conscious enough to feel any pain.

CHAPTER FORTY-ONE

WANGARI
(Phataginus tetradactyla)

Wangari saw the flash of netting coming her way and squeezed into a ball. She rocked backward, rolling with the punch as the net scooped her up. She lay on the blacktop for a moment calculating her next move. Her own scent was strong on the fibers. This was the same net that Honu had used on Mar several days earlier.

There was a sudden *thwip*. Arief grunted and fell hard onto the rock. *Enough*, Wangari thought angrily. She sprang to her hind feet, rising through the rips in the netting she had made when freeing Mar. Standing tall on Honu's blind side, Wan reached an arm across and unholstered a five-pointed tranq star from her harness strap and flung it at Honu.

Caught off guard, the sea turtle grasped at his neck with his good flipper, before flopping like a deadweight to the blacktop.

Upslope, the volcano belched liquid fire into the air. The lava river poured down into the cavities created by Mar's bomb. In the opposite direction out along the ocean's vast horizon, the pink sky appeared to be held up by great columns of cumulonimbus clouds. The water glowed yellow-green with the promise of a rising sun. And somewhere far off, from the direction of town, Wan could hear the telltale thunderous approach of a tourist helicopter racing toward the eruption.

Wan sprinted to Arief, saw that he was breathing— even stirring a little—and doubled back to check on Nukilik.

The polar bear was out cold. But Wan believed that if Arief was already fighting off sleep after one dart, the effects of two darts on Nukilik wouldn't last very long either.

"Get up," Wan urged. "Last thing we need is the

tourists sighting a polar bear out here."

Nukilik turned but didn't wake.

"What happened to Honu-u-u-u-u?" screamed a voice from above.

Wangari whipped around and looked up just in time to dive away from Mar.

The bird circled back, landed beside Honu, and nudged him with his giant yellow beak. Honu grumbled and twitched his flippers. He was still alive. Mar stooped and dislodged the laced throwing star from his comrade's throat with a flick of his beak. He straightened and glowered at Wangari. "You. You did this!"

Wan stepped forward, fiddling with her utility harness. "Yeah . . . and I'm about to do it again."

Mar cawed loudly and flapped his wings, gathering power for liftoff.

Wangari yanked out her other throwing star and flung it, but Mar ducked, and it sailed wide of its mark. "Deer droppings," she cursed in disappointment.

"Uh, is anybody coming back down here?" Murdock's voice rang in Wan's earpiece. "I'm kind of trapped."

He's stuck in Red Tail *with lava approaching!* she realized.

But Mar was rising fast. Wan knew the danger he posed. *He can't get away. . . .*

"Yoo-hoo?" Murdock pressed nervously. "Little help."

"Just a sec—" the pangolin told him. She bit her lip, calculating. . . .

She whipped out her long prehensile tongue and latched on to Mar's ankle, hoping to buy time to think. But Mar rose in fits anyway, gaining altitude quickly while the pangolin held on tight with her tongue.

"You can't bring me down," screeched the distressed bird. "Let go!"

Wan could only grunt in response.

Mar lost control for a second. But still, he circled higher and higher. "I wonder how hard you'll bounce when you hit the pavement from this hei-i-i-i-ight."

Wan was far too heavy to reel herself up by her tongue. And even if she could, what would she do when Mar's foot and her mouth met?

The approaching helicopter barreled at full speed on an intercept course, giving her an idea.

Wan felt along her belt rings until she came across her suction-cup launcher. She aimed it into the path of the approaching sound, squeezed the trigger—and tightened her tongue's grip against Mar's leg.

The suction cup hit the belly of the tourist chopper and held fast. Wan and then Mar were flung into high speed, the sudden jolt shaking Wan's radio bud out of her ear. As she reeled herself toward the chopper, Mar struggled to fly away but couldn't escape the pangolin's grasp.

The animals smacked against the bottom of the flying helicopter. Wan felt the bird's nearest shoulder muscle *pop*. Mar squawked in pain. The albatross reached with his good wing for one of the landing skids and pulled himself up onto it. Wan released her stretched tongue from his ankle and retracted it back into her mouth. She swung for the same skid, caught the metal bar with her powerful digging claws, and clambered up onto it. The suction cup launcher bumped the skid and unlatched from her belt, falling away, dangling from the belly of the chopper.

The pangolin and the albatross stood facing each other beneath a cockpit full of tourists, balanced on the landing skid of a helicopter hovering over a volcanic eruption. Mar couldn't fly away, and Wan had nowhere to go. They locked eyes and braced for combat.

"Your wing's hurt. We need to work together!" Wan urged.

"Oh, *now* you want to cooperate!"

While favoring his injury, the bird struck its beak at the pangolin. Wan danced backward.

Now what? she despaired. *This* so *isn't going to end well.*

CHAPTER FORTY-TWO

MURDOCK
(Monodon monoceros)

It took Murdock a minute to toggle the channel on his barnacle radio from *Red Tail*'s server over to the repeaters lining the lava tube. But Wan would have to switch channels on her headset too before they had a connection. Until then, the narwhal had nothing to do. Literally: nothing. With his precious interface to the outside world now fried, he was just a big fish in a slightly bigger bowl.

But then he heard it. Upslope in the lava tube, a bomb, maybe several, detonated. The water in his tank sloshed as a wave of pressure reverberated through the tube's length.

That bird blew the passage! thought Murdock. "But why?"

"Mayday! Mayday!" Wangari hollered.

"Murdock! The plume is breached. Lava pouring down below!"

Lava pouring? Where? Murdock thought with building alarm. *Wait. Down here?*

Everything suddenly made sense.

The brainies had been waiting to take advantage of this exact moment.

But what was Murdock supposed to do while trapped inside his tank?

And if their attempt to reroute the lava didn't work, and a lava river was now approaching, how in the northern lights was he supposed to escape?

"Uh, is anybody coming back down here?" Murdock inquired. "I'm kind of trapped. . . ."

He waited for a beat. Silence suffocated him.

"Yoo-hoo? Little help."

"Just a sec—" came a clipped, breathless reply. Wangari could be heard grunting with effort. There was a squawk. Another squawk. Then static. Then nothing.

"Wan?" Murdock inquired cautiously. There was no further response. "Wan?"

He would have paced if he'd had the space, or the legs. Instead, he decided to act. *I'm not waiting around.*

The narwhal executed an awkward 180 turn in his tight quarters.

The tank had a manual release that Murdock could open with his tusk. "Flush," he said, and the back plexiglass panel opened, flooding the cabin floor. Then he moved over and found the release button for the cargo ramp, clearing the way for Murdock to ride the three-day-old bathwater out of *Red Tail*.

He slid down the ramp and scraped his belly on the rough ground. "Argh! Gravity, my archnemesis, I see we meet again!" He squirmed his way across the lava tube floor, grunting and sputtering, until he parked next to the mine cart resting on the tracks nearby.

Murdock flopped himself like a fish several feet into the air. This was only a test.

He tried again, gaining momentum. Third time was the charm. He launched himself up high enough to pivot sideways in midair. He landed perfectly on top of the mine cart. It teetered briefly but then fell back into place on its tracks. Facing upslope, he used his tail to push the cart forward into the darkness of the lava tube. Seeing a bag of explosives hanging on the wall, he hooked it with his tusk and guided it down its length until it rested snugly against his upper jaw. He passed the ladder and kept shoving himself forward.

Within a minute, it felt drastically warmer than it had in the chamber with *Red Tail*. "That's not great," he said.

He'd gotten the hang of rolling the cart now and used his powerful tail muscles to fling himself forward. The heat was becoming unbearable, but he pressed on until he entered a wide portion of the tube. He was finally able to see the lava flow with his eyes.

A lumpy orange river cut across the main corridor, entering from the left and exiting through a hole on the right. The glow of molten rock illuminated the whole chamber. The current wasn't racing, but it wasn't moving slowly either. It looked deep and fluid. It flowed without interruption and without sloshing over into the main tube.

There was a problem, though.

Thanks to all his digital mapping efforts, Murdock

was perhaps more familiar with the layout of this network of tubes and tunnels than anyone.

This lava river was coursing along a route made by the brainies *before* the Endangereds had started to meddle. Murdock had clearly screwed up when instructing his team on where to dig.

He *gently* slid the satchel of bombs off his tusk and onto the ground and then blew salt water out of his blowhole to cool himself off. That was the last of the water he'd stored up.

"Does anybody copy?" he asked into his mic. "We have an issue."

"I'm here," Arief answered unexpectedly from Wan's headset. He sounded groggy. "What is it?"

Murdock cleared his cavernous throat. "I think I miscalculated, Arief. I'm sorry. But the flow seems to have diverted right into the path the brainies originally intended."

"What are you saying, Murdock?"

"This lava river is headed straight on course toward Makai Estates."

CHAPTER FORTY-THREE

ARIEF
(Pongo abelii)

Arief struggled to wake. There was a metallic taste in his mouth that he knew too well: he must have been tranqed.

The orangutan sat up too quickly and held his head. He plucked a dart from his shoulder and tossed it aside. His eyes focused just in time to register that Wangari was latched to the albatross by her long tongue. They were airborne. A helicopter was approaching their flight path from the direction of Makai Estates.

Arief rose, shaking off the last of his grogginess, and strode over to Nukilik.

"Nukilik, get up," he said. He pulled two darts from her belly and gave her a forceful shake. "We can't be spotted here."

"Huh?" She was only just starting to stir.

Arief snatched up the broken game net and covered Nuk's body with it. Then he lifted up Honu's motionless bulk and placed him on top of her too. Finally, he stretched himself out and covered her with his own body. He hoped it would provide enough camouflage over Nuk's white mass that the incoming sightseeing chopper wouldn't pay them any heed.

It sped by overhead without slowing and banked sharply to take up a circling pattern over the erupting vent in the near distance. It didn't slow and didn't seem to notice the animals.

Something small fell at Arief's feet and bounced to a halt. It was Wan's radio earbud. Arief sidled over to it, scooped it up, and shoved it into his ear.

"Does anybody copy?" Arief heard Murdock say into his ear. "We have an issue."

"I'm here," he replied. "What is it?"

Arief tried to follow as Murdock explained that he may have miscalculated, but he was finding it hard to concentrate.

"What's going on?" Nukilik asked, steadying herself on all fours. She pawed at the limp sea turtle as she gathered her bearings.

"The tunneling we've done—it's not making the difference we hoped," Arief explained. He directed his question at Murdock. "Is there anything you can do about it from where you are?"

"I have a bag of detonators," Murdock answered. "I think I can collapse the tunnel the flow is disappearing into."

"Is that safe?" Arief asked.

Murdock sighed heavily. "I'm fine, but if I block the flow toward the city . . . it'll divert into the path of least resistance. Which happens to be the main lava tube . . . which runs past *Red Tail* and into the secret bay with the tide pools and the monk seals."

Arief froze. This was a nightmare.

"What is it?" Nukilik asked him.

The orangutan pulled at his beard hairs. He met the polar bear's eyes. "We either save the town or the beach with the endangered seals."

"There's no other way?" Nuk asked.

Arief shook his head incredulously. He couldn't believe what he was about to say, but he knew in his marrow that it was the only choice. His voice was hoarse and tortured, but he gave the order in his mic. "Blow the tunnel, Murdock. Save the town."

CHAPTER FORTY-FOUR

NUKILIK
(Ursus maritimus)

"What?" Nukilik demanded. She was shocked and still groggy, and she wasn't sure that she understood. "You're choosing to rescue the humans and not the seals?"

In the distance a tourist helicopter hovered over the lava fountain, the sound of its main rotor blades competing with the roar of the lava vent.

"This isn't over yet." The orangutan showed his anger and impatience, knuckling the ground and squaring off against the polar bear. "We can airlift the seals if we have to."

"Tell Murdock to abort," Nuk insisted.

"Nuk, we found your mother! She's in Makai Estates!" Arief shouted.

Nukilik shook her head vigorously, not to say no, but to clear her mind of the last of its drowsiness. She wasn't sure what to say. And her confusion wasn't really about Atiqtalik. She hated being forced into choosing. *Another fifty-fifty scenario!* But then she realized something: a coin actually has three sides.

She stood tall with renewed excitement. "I call edge," she told the orangutan.

"What?"

"There's a third option, Arief." Nukilik rubbed her weaker paw with her stronger one while standing. "We can redirect the flow *again*. What about the charges we stashed near the mouth of the lava tube?"

"That was a last resort plan for *us*. In case we had to cover our tracks. Or in case we had to stop the brainies from escaping . . ." But he nodded, slowly at first. "Wait, though . . . Yes. Maybe your idea would work."

Nukilik felt an explosion beneath her feet. Up-slope behind Arief, the ground collapsed in a new spot, coughing up a plume of dust.

Murdock did it. But—how?

The narwhal radioed into Arief's ear.

The orangutan passed the info on to Nukilik. "That was Murdock. The flow is diverting. Get down there, make sure Murdock is okay . . . then use *Red Tail* to go get your mom. I'll divert the flow."

"No way," Nukilik said. "Your job is too dangerous to do it alone."

"Nukilik, that's an order. Someone needs to move *Red Tail* out of harm's way before I collapse the tube."

Nukilik growled, but she knew that Arief was right.

"Meanwhile, we'll get Murdock into the bay. He can start evacuating the marine life—just in case," Arief added.

Nukilik placed her tender paw on Arief's shoulder. "Thank you," she told him.

"We never leave an Endangered behind," Arief said. "That includes moms and dads too."

"Where's Wan?" the polar bear asked.

"Not clear. The bird flew off with her. But I'm on it. Now go!"

Nukilik limped off and descended the ladder.

She stepped tenderly onto the lava tube floor. It was

warmer down here than it had been before. Nukilik limped down the middle of the passage, straddling the mine cart rails on her way toward the larger chamber where *Red Tail* was parked.

"Out of the way!" trumpeted a large marine mammal from behind. Nuk turned and looked up the dark tube, confused.

Murdock materialized out of the dim light, riding a rail car at high speed. Nukilik had to jump back to miss being impaled.

"Are you okay?" she shouted, seeing only Murdock's tail shoving off the ground to propel him forward.

"Don't worry about me. The lava's coming quick. Get *Red Tail* out of here. I'm going to evacuate the tide pools."

Murdock vanished as rapidly as he had arrived, lost in the darkness of the downslope passage.

Nukilik felt a warmth at her back.

That's not right.

She turned and saw far off in the dark an orange mass rounding a bend in the corridor. "Uh oh."

With temperatures rising fast, Nuk galloped on three paws to *Red Tail*, shot up the ramp, and started pushing buttons and flipping switches. The tilt-rotor responded. It felt to Nukilik as if the aircraft was eager to get out of there too. *Red Tail* lifted up, stabilized, and shot airborne. Nukilik banked hard to the right toward Makai Estates.

After a moment, she spotted a ramshackle airstrip tucked among the tropical trees at the upper edge of town. A stand-alone white cargo trailer was parked behind the main building beside the landing strip.

"Unidentified aircraft, what's your call sign? Over."

Nukilik started at the radio, confused, and then scolded herself harshly for forgetting to turn on Wan's radar jamming equipment during the rush to take off.

"Identify yourself. You're not cleared to fly this morning. Lot of air traffic awaiting clearance already. Over."

Nukilik had no idea what to say to this guy.

"Are you experiencing an emergency? Please indicate, over. The strip you're approaching was abandoned two years ago."

"Uh—I'm fine, thank you." Nukilik tried.

"Then head due east and come into Pahoa district airfield on the other side of town at heading one, one, niner, on the double, on threat of arrest. Acknowledge, over."

Nukilik shut off the radio. *Boring conversation, anyway*, she thought.

She initiated her landing sequence, her eyes set on the cargo container at the end of the abandoned runway. "Here I come, Mamma," she promised.

CHAPTER FORTY-FIVE

ARIEF
(Pongo abelii)

***Red Tail* lifted** into view and quickly banked toward town as it continued to rise.

"Good luck, Nukilik," Arief muttered to himself. "Stay sharp."

He switched his attention to Honu. The sea turtle was clearly alive but super sleepy.

"I've reached the bay," the narwhal said over the comm. He sounded underwater.

Good, Arief thought. "I'm going to blow the fail safes," the orangutan told him. "There's a chance we can divert the flow near the mouth of the tube. But you need to evacuate the beach and the tidepools just in case."

"But what if the lava backs up and refinds the route leading to town?" said Murdock.

"Failure's not an option," Arief stated.

"All righty, then. In that case, I better go do my job."

"Copy that, big buddy. Over."

Arief looked down at Honu. The sea turtle showed signs of stirring. He pried off the artificial limb and tossed it down the shaft. The turtle was a survivor. *He'll be fine. Others may not. I have to go.*

Arief quickly found the charges they'd hidden along the topside surface of the tube.

Collapsing the tube had always been an option of last resort, but that was pretty much where things stood now.

Arief clambered over the crusty lava field, until he spotted the first of the tiny pieces of yellow flagging they'd planted in cracks to show where the explosives were hidden. A thin cable ran along the ground from there. Arief followed it back to the next bomb and repeated this until he was at the start of the sequence only several hundred feet from the edge of the sea cliffs.

The ape turned around and glanced back upslope. He found the location of the hole in the lava tube ceiling when he glimpsed Honu stumbling toward it. The turtle ducked out of view, probably on his way back into the tunnels.

What's he going back in there for? Arief worried. But he couldn't do anything about it now.

CHAPTER FORTY-SIX

HONU
(Chelonia mydas)

Descending a ladder as a sea turtle was challenging enough. But doing it with only three flippers . . . ? *This is ridiculous.*

Honu was outraged. But he was also afraid. The situation was spiraling out of his control at the worst possible moment. *I should be basking in my victory right now.*

"But no," he whined. "I'm stuck in the dark, stumbling down a rickety ladder. I'll be lucky not to wind up in the lava."

Honu grunted. He had no good options. Trying to

escape across ropy blacktop wasn't a possibility. If the sun didn't get him, the Endangereds would almost certainly catch up to him before he reached the sea or the forest.

He knew what he needed to do. There was only one way he would get out of this with his freedom intact.

Kadek.

He glanced at the approaching blob of molten rock that was pooling up and spilling over in the passage below.

A blast of hot, putrid air helped him snap into action. He slid down the rungs, toward the ground, toward his computer.

"I'm not going to die here," he decided. "I'm calling for backup." He laughed nervously, setting himself to his task.

The turtle reached the lava tube floor and ran for the chamber where *Red Tail* had been, hoping beyond hope his laptop would still be there. The tilt-rotor was gone, but his mechanical flipper was lying on the ground where Arief had tossed it. *Now, there's a nice bit of luck.* He scooped it up and fastened it to his stump, already focused on locating his computer. He used a flashlight on the artificial limb to scan the cave.

There it is!

He lunged for it, but his heart sank. *It's broken! It fell during the eruption!*

Honu tapped the power button frantically. Magically, it turned on! The screen was destroyed, but he would be able to initiate a video call by remembering the keyboard shortcuts.

The heat was getting intense.

Honu blindly navigated his computer command prompts. He hovered the tip of his flipper over the Enter key, hesitant. But he tapped it, initiating a live video conference with R.A.B.I.D. headquarters.

A shadowy, glitched-out form appeared on the broken screen. Honu knew the figure well enough to recognize him. *All right, don't panic,* he told himself. *Stay cool.* "Munson! Hey there, Munson. Can you patch me through to the Big Kahuna? It's an emergency."

"He doesn't like it when you call him that," the voice of a monitor lizard hissed out of the laptop speakers. "Kadek's in a meeting, Honu. I'll have to take a messssssssssssage."

"NO, YOU STUPID GIANT REPTILE. I have

critical intel. I need to get K on the line directly! NOW."

"That's not going to do you any favors," Munson calmly replied. "I'd watch your tone—"

"Munson, it's okay," came a new, soothing voice. "I'll take the turtle's call."

"Yesss, m'lord," said Munson.

"Route him over to my desk."

Honu felt a sudden stab of new fear. *What was I thinking?*

The image shifted, but Honu's view of what the screen was trying to show didn't improve. Blotched and glitchy, Honu couldn't make out any details of Kadek's face or whereabouts. He smiled confidently for the camera, though, in case the Big Kahuna could see him.

"This is highly irregular, Honu. Your signal better be sufficiently scrambled." The sound of a meowing cat cut Kadek off. "Hush, Cookie," he told the animal. "I'm working."

Honu took advantage of the distraction. "Kadek, I'm going to be straight with you. I was planning a real treat for you. But things have gone a bit off the rails."

The large form on-screen shifted its amorphous weight menacingly. Honu winced.

"I, um, I brought the Endangereds to the Big Island, okay?"

There was a silence. The heat inside the lava tube was getting to be unbearable. The glow of the advancing blob lit up the walls of the chamber now. The ladder in the tunnel set on fire.

"You WHAT?" Kadek thundered.

The sea turtle gulped. "I had a plan to save the monk seals here—and destroy a *town* for good measure. It was working. It might still work! But Arief . . . you wouldn't believe what that ape did, Mr. K."

"Try me," Kadek coolly invited.

"Arief chose to save the humans over the seals. I heard him say it, K. He's fighting for the humans."

The silence lingered. Honu used the break to move farther down the lava tube, buying himself time.

Finally, Kadek spoke. "Interesting, Honu. Thank you for the report. I had hoped that Arief might be willing to form an alliance. So, this is disappointing news. I'll have to deal with him. Dirty work, that."

Honu let out an explosive sigh. This was good. He had played his cards right! Kadek was pleased.

"It won't be easy. The Endangereds are a smart team,"

Honu warned. "But I can share some insight into—"

"Oh, don't you worry your half shell about it, Honu. I know just how to approach this situation."

"What about me?" the turtle ventured to ask. "Things are getting a bit hot down here. Where should I go for extraction?"

The figure on the other end of the botched live feed laughed mirthlessly. "Honu. I appreciate your report, but I have to get ready! Put certain things in motion. You're on your own, now, I'm afraid."

"What? Wait! Kadek, please—"

The transmission cut out, leaving Honu alone as the intense heat gathered. He gulped in the sudden darkness, and watched as the walls pulsed red around him.

CHAPTER FORTY-SEVEN

ARIEF
(Pongo abelii)

Arief surveyed the situation one last time. The detonators were armed and ready. To the northwest the lava fountain continued to spew vog—volcanic fog—as two more tourist helicopters approached the area.

We're on full display out here. We've got to wrap this up.

Satisfied that he had no other choice at this point, Arief pushed the countdown button and galloped away as fast as he could.

But after a minute, nothing detonated.

Arief surveyed the lava field. He pulled at his beard

and radioed Murdock. "Hey, I tried blowing the line, but nothing happened."

"Uh-oh," said Murdock. "There must be a short."

Arief grunted. The timer was stuck at zero and now he had to race back *toward* the explosives?

The orangutan spotted a patch of trees growing out of a section of sharp *a'a*. It was in line with the string of bombs and seemed a likely spot to find the cable severed. He crept as lightly but quickly as he could out among the sharp rocks.

The break was visible in the center of the patch. "Found it," he reported to Murdock. "I just strip the wire and twist tie them back together?"

"That should do it," answered Murdock, who was clearly dealing with his own unknown problems while taking the time to respond. "But the detonations will start immediately. Make sure you can get out of there."

"Doesn't really matter—" Arief said gravely. "Time's up."

He cut into both ends of the cable with his teeth and peeled away the rubber sheathing. Then he twisted the ends together. Electricity jolted through his fingers, but it was nothing compared to the explosions that he could instantly feel advancing toward him.

Arief rushed over the a'a, cutting his feet and his fingers on the sharp, jagged ground, trying to outrace the approaching cave-in.

But he already knew: he wasn't going to make it.

CHAPTER FORTY-EIGHT

WANGARI
(Phataginus tetradactyla)

The tour helicopter hovered high over a lava-spewing chasm.

Balanced atop the landing skid, Wangari wiped her brow. Heat pulsed against the chopper's belly as Wan faced off against the injured albatross.

Mar gripped the landing skid with his good wing while Wan held on with her long prehensile tail.

The lava boiled bright red out of its hole below them.

"Stay back!" Mar warned.

"Let me help you, Mar," pleaded Wangari.

The albatross hissed. "Why would I ever trust you?"

Wan furled her brow in disgust, her anger matched by an explosive burp of liquid rock from below. "You were trying to destroy a whole town!"

"Trying?" mocked the albatross. "It's done! There's no stopping what has begun!"

"You're wrong," Wan said. She tried to sound confident, but maybe she was only convincing herself. "We tricked you. We did all the drilling where *we* wanted to drill."

Mar hissed again, hugging his bar tight. He coughed and spat out something plastic that fell out of sight and burnt up instantly in the lava river below. "I was right about you. Honu wouldn't listen, but I was right."

"Tell me who's behind all this. Who's *really* in charge?" Wan asked. "You could have been one of us."

Mar shrank back another step, and one of his webbed feet lost its footing for a second. "I'll never join you!" he shrieked.

"What is R.A.B.I.D.?" demanded Wangari, taking another step closer.

"How do you know about that?"

"Murdock found a folder on your hard drive."

Mar's face contorted. The anger vanished and was replaced by fear. "You're not supposed to know about that. We failed." He looked down at the gushing rent as if actually contemplating a leap.

"No! Don't!" shouted Wan. She loosened the grip of her tail and dove forward to stop the bird from letting go.

Instead of letting go, Mar pecked Wan with his beak. Wan couldn't dodge the attack, but her scales absorbed the blow. She lost her balance and toppled off the landing skid.

She acted fast, latching her tongue to the skid, and she used the momentum of her fall to swing back up onto the rail and plant her feet firmly in place again.

Mar screamed his frustration. He was about to say something else when a fit of coughing overtook him, and he hacked up a half-digested baby pacifier—and then he accidentally breathed it back in.

The plastic garbage lodged his windpipe. The albatross gripped at his neck with his weak wing. He gave Wan a desperate look, gurgled, and then passed out.

"Mar!" Wangari shouted. She watched, stunned in silent horror, as the albatross fell from the helicopter's skid. The giant white bird tumbled through the air

302

toward the lava fountain.

Wan reached toward the helicopter's belly for her dangling suction cup device, but she couldn't get to it. There was no time. Mar was falling fast. She didn't think; she dove.

Wan bulleted toward the fiery lake.

Her aim was true. She slammed into Mar's flailing body, and she gripped him tight. She turned him around, mounted his back, and pulled open his wings. The pair entered a flat spin. It was hot. The volcanic eruption spun in circles, growing larger. Wangari yanked up with her strong claws against Mar's extended left wing. Their freefall stabilized into actual flight.

Wangari passed back across the rift, using the thermal column to gain some lift, and then she slingshotted wide of the danger and out toward the sea. She gathered her bearings and miraculously spotted the shaft where *Red Tail* had been. She piloted the unconscious albatross toward it.

Wangari's landing was intentionally brutal. They smacked down hard. Wan tumbled off the bird's back and over the blacktop. At the same time, the bird's lungs flattened, and he coughed out the baby pacifier.

Wangari sprang to her feet just in time to catch the object arching through the air.

The albatross sat up, coughing first, cradling his aching stomach, before falling back, moaning in defeat.

Wan tossed the pacifier at the bird. "You're welcome," she said.

"What haa-a-a-aappened?" Mar croaked.

"You and I had a falling-out," Wan answered with a sarcastic smile. "But I think we managed to find some common ground."

Mar squawked in protest, but Wan couldn't understand him. His vocal cords were shot.

Wan wondered what to do with the wheezing bird, but before she came up with a plan, she heard a familiar voice shout: "Wan! Run!"

The pangolin spun around and spotted Arief, who was knuckle-galloping toward them.

She felt a massive explosion beneath her feet and then saw the ground collapsing behind the orangutan.

And like that, Arief was swallowed whole from Wangari's view.

CHAPTER FORTY-NINE

MURDOCK
(Monodon monoceros)

After helping Arief figure out the problem with the detonators, Murdock turned his attention to rounding up the monk seals.

The lava tube ceiling collapsed far away upslope, but the commotion it caused was detectible from the water.

The monk seals slid into the pool from the small black sand beach where they'd been sunning themselves. They swarmed the narwhal like a playful school of five-hundred-pound fish.

Murdock sounded the alarm. "Lava's flowing this way. We need to evacuate the tide pools!"

"Are you a deformed hammerhead?" one of them asked.

Murdock sputtered. "No. I'm not a shark. I'm a whale."

"We know the whales around here," another seal insisted. "You don't look like any of 'em."

I don't have time for this!

"Are you a marlin?" asked monk seal number three.

The questions kept coming. "A swordfish?"

"No. I'm not a *fish*. I'm a MAMMAL."

"Where are your whiskers?"

"Don't even start with that," Murdock warned.

"Maybe he's a teenage humpback that had a boating accident?" one of them suggested. "Is that stick stuck in your head?"

The seven seals chattered excitedly at that idea. Several of them reached out and touched Murdock's tusk, which would have earned most animals a sharp poke under normal circumstances.

Murdock sighed, thoroughly humiliated at this point. "That's exactly right! I'm a teenage humpback that had a boating accident. Can we go now?"

"Poor thing," the seals agreed.

"Guys?" Murdock tried to redirect their enthusiasm. "Lava . . ."

"Is it coming here?"

"Yes! It's coming quickly. Spread the word, okay? Every turtle, fish, eel. Every urchin, every octopus—they all need to file for the exits."

A young pair of the seals stiffened to attention and took the challenge to heart. They raced off to warn the entire tide pool community.

"How big is your colony, total?" Murdock asked the remaining seals. "I need to make sure you're all safe."

Amid several interruptions and some repeat questions about whether he was sure he wasn't really a hammerhead, Murdock managed to ascertain that the colony consisted of twelve seals. These seven individuals had been hanging around the tide pools and the small beach all morning, and the other five were out either hunting down breakfast or patrolling the coast for predator sharks.

As the seals chattered, Murdock swam up to the lava tube as close as he could get. He could feel the heat from the approaching blob, and he could smell some pretty nasty gases wafting out of the cave mouth. The lava was advancing slowly but steadily, growing new tentacles of glowing orange-red arms. The noise coming from the tube reminded Murdock of the sounds of a pile of broken glass being swept into a dustpan.

As soon as the lava reached the mouth of the cave, the water near the entry point would instantly boil and the steam would mix with the supercooling lava to form laze, the deadly combination of gases and microscopic shards of glass that would destroy the lungs of any wildlife who breathed it in. And of course, any marine life in the immediate area would boil alive.

And that would be the end for these tide pools.

"Come on, you sea dogs, let's get a move on!" he urged the three seals still crowded around him.

"This beach was so nice and quiet," the eldest of them answered.

"I'm sorry," Murdock said. "We're trying to save it. But just in case we don't, we need to evacuate."

"If the beach is gone, we'll have to head back up the northwestern chain to a quieter island somewhere," one of the elder seals said.

"If we can stop this lava in time," Murdock suggested,

"you should stay here. You guys are protected under the Endangered Species Act. If the humans see that you live here, they'll protect you along with the other marine wildlife in the area."

"That was the plan all along!" a familiar and nefarious reptilian snarled. It was Honu. "Why'd you ruin everything?"

Murdock followed the voice. The evil green sea turtle was standing on the ledge of lava tube mouth. His eye patch was slightly off-kilter. The utility arm was fastened with a *harpoon* attachment.

That's not good, Murdock thought nervously. He turned to the seals in the water beside him. "Go!" he told them. "Save everyone you can. Get them back from the cliffs!"

The monk seals seemed to get it. They darted off and began rounding up stragglers in the coral nearest the lava's eminent entry point.

"You chose to save the humans over your fellow animals," Honu screamed. "You Endangereds disgust me."

"I've had enough of your shell games, Honu!" Murdock shouted back. "You're not looking for solutions. You only want to make the *news*."

"That's a lie," the reptile hissed.

"None of your schemes are about helping monk seals, or pygmy sloths, or biodiversity. Your only aim is to impress the folks at R.A.B.I.D. And what's their bottom line, Honu? Mother Nature only knows."

Honu gasped. "You *were* reading my computers!" He barked his fury and pointed the harpoon at Murdock.

As terrified as he suddenly was, the narwhal didn't flinch. "You're not going to murder me, Honu. I don't buy it. If you pull that trigger, you're only proving my point. You've lost your way. You're crossing a line. You already have."

After a moment of tense hesitation, Honu lowered his harpoon arm with a snarl of frustration. Murdock had called his bluff. "The *point* was to deliver your rag-tag team into Mr. K's hands."

"Mr. K?"

"Panama was just a shadowing exercise. Gather intel. Report back. Blah, blah, blah. But I knew we could do better. You're my ticket to upper management. And I will hook you and reel you in if that's what it takes."

Rocks rained from the ceiling of the lava tube above Honu. Murdock winced. Arief's upslope explosions had

310

probably destabilized the roof all the way out here.

"Hey, Flipper," Murdock warned Honu.

"What?" the reptile spat. "Don't call me that!"

"You better flip."

Honu looked up and scoffed. He turned back to Murdock and cast him an evil eye. "Nice try, but I'm not falling for your—"

The ceiling gave way. Boulders and great slabs of basalt rained down, collapsing into the tube.

Honu cried out in surprise, stumbled, then fell into the lagoon.

Murdock ducked below the surface. He saw the sea turtle coming at him, surprisingly nimble in the water. "I spared you!" he raged. "I won't make that mistake again!"

The sharpened point of his harpoon glistened, pointed straight between Murdock's eyes.

CHAPTER FIFTY

NUKILIK
(Ursus maritimus)

Nukilik peeked around the corner of the cargo hold and took a good, long look to make sure the area was clear. *Red Tail* was parked only a few feet away, nestled and out of sight between the abandoned building of the old airstrip and a dense forest. She had seen tourist helicopters approaching from town. A newer airport must exist on the far side of Makai Estates. Pahoa district airfield, maybe? And that was part of the problem with these humans, wasn't it? Nukilik didn't understand why this old facility couldn't have just been updated, instead of being abandoned entirely for something newer only a few miles away.

But for now, she was grateful this place was quiet and empty of people.

Empty of *people*, yes. But not animals. *Watch out for more brainies*, she warned herself. *Honu and Mar can't be operating alone.*

Nuk ventured forward to access the doors of the steel container she'd spied from the air. She heard a generator. The roof of the hold had a cooling unit. *Yep, Mamma has to be inside.*

The double doors of the cargo hold were locked with a big chain and padlock. She swiped angrily at the chain. It gave way on the second attempt. Her stomach filled with nervous energy, and she pulled the doors open from both sides, hit by a wall of cold, dry air.

Atiqtalik was there, alone.

She had been sleeping in the far corner, but now she stirred and looked toward Nuk.

"Mamma!" Nukilik shouted. She rushed into the container, which rocked on its coil springs.

Atiqtalik growled weakly but seemed to recognize her daughter. "Nukilik?"

"It's me, Mamma. Are you okay?"

"I'm stiff. But a big white gull comes with fish each day."

"That's it?"

The elder polar bear nodded.

"Well, let's get you out of here."

She heard the faint whine of sirens approaching and remembered back to her unfortunate chat with the air traffic controller. "Mamma, we need to go, now."

"Where is this place?" Atiqtalik wanted to know.

Nukilik remembered back to her journey from the Arctic to the Galápagos, to her feelings of confusion from before she became hyper. She had a great deal of sympathy for her mom's questions—but there was no time to answer them. "I will try to explain it all, Mamma. But I can't yet. You have to trust me and follow me. *Now.*"

"I'm not going anywhere until I know what is happening."

"Mamma, I'm not going to argue. Either you come with me willingly, or I will carry you out."

"I am your elder, Nukilik—"

Exasperated, Nuk reared up and roared.

Atiqtalik shrank back in fear and yielded.

"I stake my claim, Atiqtalik, for the right to lead," she told her mother. "It is time for the elders to listen to the wisdom of their youth!" she commanded. "Follow me and I will make you safe!"

Atiqtalik stared up at her daughter with a hard expression. And then she relented and looked away. She rose, bowing to Nukilik before meeting her eyes again. And then she followed her daughter out of the cargo hold, across the unkempt patch of grasses and crumbling tarmac, and into *Red Tail*'s cabin.

The sirens were drawing closer. Nukilik was certain they were coming here.

"What's going on? What are those noises?" Atiqtalik asked, worried.

Nukilik hushed her. "You're in good paws, Mother. You're going home."

Police vehicles were visible now, coming in a line at high speed across the far end of the abandoned airstrip. Nuk fired up the propellers, remembering to turn on the radar stealth mode this time. Within seconds of the first cop car's arrival, Nukilik was airborne and soaring to new heights.

CHAPTER FIFTY-ONE

WANGARI
(Phataginus tetradactyla)

When the lava tube collapsed, taking Arief with it, Wan sprang forward. She had to help even if it meant leaving Mar behind.

"Arief!"

She reached the edge of the deep trench newly carved out of the Earth's crust and saw that the lava tube was gone, buried under a pile of rubble. Upslope, the tube was intact, and lava from the eruption flowed from its depths, only to be dammed by the cave-in. A molten orange pool was forming, its heat rising in gusts toward

Wan as if she stood at the lip of a smokestack.

"The active flow," she said, processing what she was seeing. *It would've poured out into the tide pools taking Murdock and the seals with him if Arief hadn't blown the entire fail-safe array.* "He stopped it!" *For now.*

She backed a step away. The heat and the noxious gases were too much. But she couldn't leave. Worriedly, she circled the trench looking for Arief.

The dust cleared out. Something stirred among the top layer of crumbled black rock. A lanky, hairy arm emerged. Wangari's eyes focused on Arief, struggling without success to pull himself up and out of the debris. "You're alive!"

"Stay back." He coughed. "It's too hot!"

Wangari ignored his warnings and scrambled down the rubble slope to where he was lodged. "I'm stuck," he said. He locked eyes with Wan, too afraid to say anything more.

Wan was afraid too.

She dug into the wreckage with her highly adapted claws, but it was no use. She was far too small to move the large slabs of basalt pinning Arief down.

From somewhere out of sight, Wan heard a chopper

approach. The tour guide pilot had probably caught a glimpse of the long cave-in and was flying closer to give the passengers more for their money.

"Complete your mission," Arief ordered. "Get out of here, Wan. There's nothing to be done."

"I'm not leaving you," Wan said, digging despite the fact that she was getting nowhere.

"Wan, we knew the risks. These fumes are poison. You need to go."

"No—" she answered. "We leave no animal behind!" She glanced toward the pooling lava, still meters below but rising.

"So, why don't we take him with us, then?"

Arief and Wan looked toward the lip of the cave-in.

Nukilik stood against the blue sky at the edge of the drop off. The aircraft Wan had been hearing was *Red Tail*!

"Nukilik, you're a sight for sore eyes!" Wangari shouted. "Hurry! Time's running out!"

Nukilik looked back behind her shoulder. "Give me just a second."

To Wan's dismay, Nuk disappeared but returned less than thirty seconds later with Atiqtalik by her side.

Nuk issued a sharp command. She and her mother descended the crumbled embankment. Nukilik was light on her broken paw, wincing with each step as she searched out the most stable path. Atiqtalik arrived first. She sniffed at the air and regarded Arief and Wan suspiciously.

"Lift that, if you can," Nuk told her mother.

The elder polar bear eyed her daughter but obeyed, prying at the slab of basalt trapping Arief in place. She wasn't strong enough to lift it on her own.

A sudden gush of liquid rock came down the tube, crashing with an actual wave against the fiery pool. The molten surface lapped up against the debris and stuck like goo, before hardening into black stone.

Something had clearly dislodged upstream, and the lava spilled now much more rapidly into the open chamber. The pool rose quickly. The heat was nearly unbearable for Wan.

Arief hissed in fear or maybe pain. Wangari barked in worried sympathy. How long would it be before the lava seeped into the rubble?

"Hurry," Wan urged.

Nuk raced around the debris pile to the far side of

the slab, opposite her mother. They lifted the heavy stone together. Still, the effort wasn't enough. Nukilik took several deep breaths in a row, pushed with her back and all four of her limbs. With a cry of agony and effort, it was enough. Arief was free!

Lava oozed nearer, hot, crackling, and exploding, sounding like glass constantly being shattered.

Wangari darted into the opening that Nuk had created. She dug at the debris, tearing at the rocks snagged into Arief's hair. The orangutan cried out in pain as he pulled his bleeding legs free of rubble. He and Wan scrambled to safety.

The slab crashed back down. Arief lay upon the jumble of rocks for a moment, covered in cuts and scrapes.

"We have to go!" Nukilik barked. She cradled her paw, which was noticeably swollen.

"You don't say?" Arief managed between heavy breaths. He glanced at the rising lava pool and struggled painfully to all fours. "Lead the way!"

The animals raced up the sharp rock and filed into the tilt-rotor. Arief made a slight detour, veering over to the spot where Mar lay gasping. He dragged the giant bird on board and strapped him into a seat. Mar looked cross and exhausted.

"You're not going to make a fuss?" Arief asked the albatross.

The bird attempted an answer but couldn't muster a sound.

"I'll eat you, if you don't stay put," Nukilik threatened while rapidly punching buttons and firing up the engines.

Mar frowned and tried to cross his wings, but his sprained wing wouldn't fold the way he'd wanted it to.

"He's hoarse," Wan explained. "But he knows he's safer with us than waiting for R.A.B.I.D."

"Can you fly her?" Arief asked Nukilik, glancing a bit nervously between the two polar bears.

"I'm fine," Nukilik answered, flipping a final series of switches with her good front paw. "Several days of jackhammering with a broken hand catches up with you in the end, I suppose. You okay, Mother?"

"I'm very nervous," Atiqtalik admitted. "But I trust you." She gave Nukilik a long, prideful look and left it at that, resting her chin on the floor of the cabin and shutting her eyes as if wishing for all this excitement to go away.

As the propellers gathered speed, Nukilik reached for a medical kit and rummaged through it. "Just take a small bite of this," she told her mother. "It'll calm your nerves."

The old polar bear listened to her daughter and ate the sedative Nukilik offered.

A trio of helicopters appeared then, circling above *Red Tail*.

"Ignore them," said Arief. "I want an aerial look at the flow."

Red Tail rose. The hovering choppers fell back, making room. An explosion of lava from the original vent rained fire down on the area, and the tourist copters retreated farther for safety.

"Stay here for a minute," said Arief.

The Endangereds took a long look at the lava pool rising against the collapsed ceiling of the cave-in. Wan wasn't sure which direction it would spill out once it got high enough. She also wasn't sure what they could possibly do about it now, anyway, if they weren't satisfied with the direction it was taking.

"Look! Look!" cried Nukilik. "It's working. It's back-flowing out of the tunnels *we* excavated!"

A quarter mile to the east, toward the town of Makai Estates, but still far short of its boundary—and significantly closer to the coast—lava spurted and sputtered out of a crack in the blacktop. The new fountain of material slopped against the ground and funneled toward the cliffs where it would drop into the sea exactly where the Endangereds had always hoped it would.

"Now that's how you reroute!" Arief exclaimed, overjoyed and relieved.

Mar hissed.

They hovered above the lava fields, drifting slowly toward the new spout, and surveyed the landscape for a couple minutes.

"Who's on the line with Murdock?" Wangari asked. "Is he okay?"

"I had him on my comm until I fell in," said Arief. "Let's get over to the lagoon and scoop him up."

"No more sightseeing," agreed Nukilik. "Looks like that's a wrap. But what about Honu?"

Mar offered another squawk of disgust but couldn't formulate his protest into words.

"I saw that reptile crawl back into his hole as the lava was pushing forward through the tube," said Arief. "He had nowhere to go but toward the sea. I'll bet you a month's worth of chores that Murdock has him well under control by now."

CHAPTER FIFTY-TWO

MURDOCK
(Monodon monoceros)

Honu aimed his harpoon at Murdock and fired.

"One for all and all for one!" Murdock parried the blow with his tusk and batted the harpoon out of the way.

Honu gurgled, furious, and charged the narwhal.

"Really?" Murdock said. He whacked Honu with his tusk, but Honu turned and shielded himself with his shell. He dog-rolled and swooped to the pool floor upside down, coming in for an attack from below. Murdock whipped his tail at his assailant and surprised himself by connecting squarely with the turtle's half shell. Honu went tumbling back as if struck by a cannonball.

His appendage came loose and sank to the sandy channel floor.

Honu darted away, still remarkably fast. Murdock gave chase, readying his tusk for a knockout blow to the head. But Honu slipped through a crevice of rock decorated with colorful corals. Murdock had no prayer of following the turtle into that tight of a space.

A quick inspection convinced Murdock that the coral had only one opening. There was no escape for the slippery troublemaker.

"Honu! Come out of there. It's over."

"Make me," the reptile spat back.

No chance of that. Murdock would have to lose approximately five hundred pounds first.

He tried thrusting his tusk into the closed space but was rewarded only with a sharp, *painful* coral scrape to his forehead. "Ow!" he griped.

"That's what you get. Go away!"

What do I do now? he wondered. *Wait him out?* This made Murdock laugh. He could hold his breath for about twenty minutes. Sea turtles could rest underwater for several *hours* before needing to surface. *This standoff might last awhile.*

"Orange leader, do you copy?"

Murdock's mic check received no response. This was concerning, but he also thought he could hear *Red Tail's* signature twin propellers somewhere above the water in the distance.

The minutes stretched on. Murdock surfaced just quickly enough to steal a glimpse of the lava tube. The cave-in seemed to be doing its job. There was no evidence that lava was oozing through the cracks.

He ducked back down to keep watch over his cornered prey while he tried to figure out his next move.

"Murdock, do you copy?"

It was Nukilik. And by the clear, crisp sound of her voice, she was radioing from *Red Tail's* cockpit.

"Loud and bubbly, old buddy!"

"What's your status? . . . And *don't* say endangered."

"I've got Honu cornered, but he's hunkered down in the coral. I can't reach him. Over."

"The lava appears to be hardening against the cave-in. It's backflowing through the diversionary tunnels now."

Murdock fizzed with relief.

"We're coming. We have to act fast. Fish that slimy reptile out of hiding. And then be ready for upload."

A pair of monk seals suddenly flanked Murdock. "That's everybody," they reported proudly. "The pools are evacuated."

Murdock was encouraged to hear that. "It looks like we averted the worst. But keep the whole community back and safe until we know for sure. Meanwhile, any ideas how to fish out that last sea turtle hiding in there? He's injured and hallucinating." Murdock laughed to himself.

"Forget you," Honu grumbled from his shadowy crevice.

"Injured! We're on it!" the seals agreed. With puppy-doglike enthusiasm they set to their task of "rescuing" the poor sea turtle from his hiding spot. They swam down into the grotto, avoiding the sharpest coral snags.

Murdock heard a brief struggle. The sea turtle cursed. And before long, Honu emerged, escorted on either side by monk seals that were very pleased with themselves.

Murdock pressed in on his foe, pushing the tip of his tusk up against Honu's neck while crowding him against

a coral wall. "One move and I'll practice my spearfishing skills, you hear me?"

Honu's eye narrowed, but he relented. "You have Mar in custody?"

Murdock wasn't sure but he faked it. "You might as well surrender together until we can figure out what to do."

Honu sighed in defeat.

"Want me to fish that weird metal flipper off the floor?" a seal asked.

"No. Leave it," Murdock instructed. "It's dangerous."

The water darkened above. Murdock held Honu at tusk-point while he gazed up with one eye. *Red Tail* descended directly over their position. A net fell into the water, and the narwhal instructed the seals to help him secure Honu with it.

"Really? You're treating me like bycatch?"

"Just taking out the trash." The narwhal winked.

"Thank you for your help," Murdock told the seals.

"No. Thank you! You saved our home," one of the seals acknowledged. "We can stay here now."

"Any time an animal's in danger," Murdock promised, "the Endangereds are here to help."

The seals playfully circled Murdock and Honu a few times and then went to rest on the beach. Murdock towed his grumpy bycatch out through the channel to deeper waters, where *Red Tail* initiated procedures to bring him and a boatful of seawater on board.

As the intake process was completed, a trio of helicopters appeared again over the bluff at the top of the cliffs and hovered there like ominous sentries.

"They won't follow us, will they?" asked Nukilik.

"Not out to sea," Wan assured her. "The Coast Guard might, though. Let's jet before they arrive!"

"How's our fuel?" Arief wondered aloud.

"We can make it to the Aleutian Islands of Alaska," Wan said. "We'll be good. We're going to have to find a docking station once we get that far, though, before finishing the straight-line shot across the pole over toward Baffin Bay."

"Make it so," said Arief.

With a crowd of seven on board, *Red Tail* set sail high over the sea, banking due north.

CHAPTER FIFTY-THREE

NUKILIK
(Ursus maritimus)

Baffin Bay, Greenland

Nukilik and her mother crossed the great alluvial plain. Windswept snowdrifts and vast but dwindling patches of hardpack stretched across their path. Nukilik led the way, and it seemed at times that only one set of pawprints marked their passage over the snow.

The daughter-and-mother pair spied their destination at last: a sleuth of polar bears gathered on a rocky slope down by the sea. They lazed on a thick sheet of ice worn through in spots, where seawater rippled as pools. Nuk knew very well they were waiting for seals to come up for breath here, and then they would each play their assigned roles in the food web established over the course of eons.

"Nukilik, I am not sure about this."

"I know you're not, Mother. But I am."

The two of them descended the slope to the pebbled shore, and a familiar male polar bear with a confident gait intercepted them. "You will go now," he challenged Nukilik. "This is our hunting ground—"

The Endangered made her move. She bared her teeth, reared up to her full standing height, and swiped her healthy paw at the young male with enough force to snap a chain. The stunned polar bear stumbled back, almost fell over, and then stood his ground, gawking.

With the others near the pools fully at attention, the young male considered his options and unwisely chose to meet Nukilik's challenge with an attack of his own. He bounded toward her, snarling. But Nuk stood in his path like a granite boulder. She roared her warning and puffed her chest. When the other bear lunged in to take her down, Nukilik batted him away instead, and this time he did lose his balance and fell to the polished rocks.

Nukilik's broken paw secretly throbbed with pain, but no one here would ever know.

The polar bear stooped his head and backed away, uncertain but very much still calculating his next move.

"I claim the right to rule this feeding ground," Nukilik declared, loudly so that all could hear. "I am Nukilik, daughter of Atiqtalik. I am the one who is strong, and strongest among you all."

The male polar bear bared his teeth but didn't dare spring forward.

"But I shall surrender that claim," Nukilik continued. "I will not stay here. If you will recognize Atiqtalik, and never deny her equal access to these waters, you will not see me again."

The male polar bear looked between everyone in the sleuth and finished by locking eyes with Nukilik before finally glancing away. "I accept," he said quietly.

Nukilik stood down. Privately, she exploded with relief. But she maintained a confident exterior. "Good," she told the male. "Leave us to say goodbye, and then I shall retreat."

The polar bears drifted back.

"You are very strong, Nukilik," Mother said. "Have

I ever told you that?"

"Yes, and I know it's true because you say it's so."

"Have I ever told you how proud I am of you?"

Nukilik did not answer. She was suddenly fighting back tears.

"The life you lead is not one I understand, Nukilik," Mother said. "But I see that you do it with courage. That is what matters. The Old Ways don't suit you, and your New Ways guide you to a place I cannot follow."

"Mother—" Nukilik tried to say.

"I will miss you, Nukilik. I will not forget you as I had once started to. Thank you for saving me, and for being my daughter."

"I will visit you, Mother," Nukilik promised.

"And I will be here . . . always," she replied. "Even when I am gone, I will be with you. Watching down upon you among the old Natures to guide you."

Nukilik and her mother nuzzled noses. Atiqtalik kissed away her daughter's tears and departed. As Nuk sat and watched, her mother made her way along the snowy coast against a vast and beautiful landscape, slowly fading out of sight.

When she could no longer see her mother, Nuk lifted

herself onto her three good paws and made her way back to *Red Tail*, to her waiting family of misfits, and to the uncertain times ahead. But she took solace in the certain knowledge, at least, that saving endangered animals was her forever calling.

CHAPTER FIFTY-FOUR

ARIEF
(Pongo abelii)

The Galápagos Islands, Ecuador

The Endangereds settled back at the Ark. Another visit from Dr. Fellows and Mr. Gooding and their crews began and concluded without incident, and Arief agreed to reward the gang with a bit of long overdue "shore leave."

"Time for that luau we never got in Hawai'i!" Murdock trumpeted.

And now here they were, on one of the most secluded beaches in the entire world, soaking up some well-earned rays.

Arief and Nukilik wore sunglasses while lounging on adjustable beach chairs stolen from the Ark's cafeteria patio. A table was anchored in the sand between them, topped with colorful drinks capped with tiny rainbow umbrellas. Nukilik had her paw in a sling and the pair listened to Hawaiian music on portable speakers.

A flock of blue-footed boobies waddled along the shore, somewhat shattering the illusion that this was Hawaii, but Wangari was out on the waves on a surfboard beside Murdock, teaching herself how to surf. She was getting the hang of it, but she and Murdock came ashore for a break.

The narwhal slid up onto the beach. "We should train outside the dome more often."

"Training, huh? We should have more luaus," Wan amended, parking her board beside the whale.

"I keep thinking about our new guests," said Murdock. "Should we let them out for some sun?"

"Guests? You mean prisoners," Nukilik insisted.

Honu and Mar were being held in secure underground cages nearby. Arief *hmph*ed. "I don't think they've proven they can behave yet. It may be a while, to be honest."

"Do you think they'll talk?" asked Nukilik. "We need to find out more about R.A.B.I.D. They're still our only lead so far."

"Mar might start talking eventually," Arief surmised. "Once his voice is back. Who knows? Honu's pretty bitter, and I don't see that changing. He's afraid of something, though. More afraid of it than he is of us. Maybe we'll get him to talk by offering him our protection. I don't know. We'll need to decide soon what to do with them."

"Catch and release?" Nukilik said doubtfully.

"We'll see," said Arief. "They're dangerous in the wild. But they may represent a threat to us, here. What if Fellows stumbles across them?"

"Not on my watch. Hey, look," said Nukilik, scrolling down a news article on her smartphone. "The vent that opened up while we were on the Big Island finally cut off today. The flow's not entering the ocean anymore. It's official, gang: the town and the secluded beach have *both* been spared."

"Can you imagine if that much lava had poured into Makai Estates?" asked Wan. They all sat in silence listening to the chatter of the blue-footed boobies as they thought about their win.

"I want to share an observation," Murdock announced. "It's been on my mind. I might as well bounce it off you. Those monk seals, they really stepped up when I asked them for some teamwork. I don't think they would have been that helpful to the rest of the tide-poolers on their own."

Arief nodded. He'd been considering this phenomenon too. While animals usually didn't naturally help each other during disasters, something about the Endangereds had gotten them to cooperate.

"What do you suppose is behind that?" Murdock asked.

"Even my mom seemed to have a slightly clearer understanding of immediate things when she was around us," Nukilik pointed out.

"The sloth too," agreed Wan. "I wonder if this is subtly tied into how Quag was able to control a prairie dog colony. Maybe we do have an open wavelength with normal animals, as hypers."

"Possibly," Arief concluded. "We will have to investigate further. What's far more troubling is this brainy directive we're learning about. Honu and Mar. And Quag too—they're not alone out there, are they?"

"We'll get to the bottom of it, Arief," said Wan.

"Meanwhile, I'm going to get to the bottom of the bay!" Murdock announced. "Race you to the water!"

It was a challenge the narwhal lost. Wan jumped up and shoved her surfboard, borrowed from the crew quarters, into the water before Murdock had even completed his 180 turn on the sand. "Best two out of three?" he joked.

Arief watched his teammates enjoy the surf; then he gazed out at the open ocean. He was hopeful that a new era of cooperation and stability was approaching, and that understanding between the needs of humans and wildlife could be achieved. But there were unmistakable thunderclouds out on the horizon. And the orangutan knew that more preparations were needed for when the storm rolled in. Until then, the Endangereds would remain on call. They would take every action needed. And they would be prepared for anything.

Or so Arief thought.

EPILOGUE

KADEK

(Pongo abelii)

As Arief gazed out at the sea from the comfort of his lounging chair, Kadek watched him through a pair of powerful binoculars, hiding in the shoreline bushes down the beach.

"See, Munson. I told you they'd come here."

The monitor lizard kept shifting his feet around, trying to avoid the heat of the sand. This amused Kadek for some reason.

"Are we going to rescue Honu and Mar? With the Endangereds on the beach, we could infiltrate—"

"We don't *do* rescues, Munson."

"Yes, m'lord."

"It's beneath us. That turtle is ambitious. He'll work twice as hard to earn my respect now. Why would I deny him the opportunity?"

"But they're off their supply, m'lord. It may change their abilities—"

"Don't point out the obvious to me. I understand that. I also understand how it works with the Endangereds here at the Ark too. What I'm hoping to learn is what kind of overlap there is. We're able to conduct an experiment here, Munson. One method pitted against the other."

"I see, m'lord."

"Don't grovel, Munson. It's unbecoming, even for a lizard."

"Yes, m'lord. Sorry, m'lord. I mean . . . sorry again, m'lord."

Kadek released a deep, resigned sigh. "Slither off and ready the sub. I need to clear my thoughts."

The lizard stiffened expectantly. "Are you . . . going to reveal yourself to him now?" He hurried to justify his question: "I only ask because I wouldn't want to miss it.

You wouldn't deny me the look on his face, would you, m' . . . sir?"

Kadek turned to face his servant. "I appreciate your awareness that the moment before us is, in fact, momentous. I will remember your enthusiasm, Munson. But what happens next must unfold carefully. It's a delicate thing. And I want the blow, when it comes, to not only be convincing, but morally devastating. I don't want to outplay Arief, Munson. I want to demolish him."

"Delicious, m'lord."

"We must send a message to all his ilk, to all those animals that would take the Endangereds' side in the battle ahead: having a soft spot for the humans is the road to ruin. I will not tolerate it. And Arief, above all others, should know better."

Kadek bared his teeth and suppressed a growl that might have carried on the wind. He was surprised at his own sudden flood of anger. If he was going to go forward with his new plan, he would have to learn to control his emotions around his brother.

"Yes," he said aloud, not so much to Munson, but to all the world. "When we finally meet again . . . when I tell him just who I am . . . and when I share our memories of the moment when our mother died at the hands of those poachers all those years ago . . . I want him to embrace me. He'll cry on my shoulder. I want to see the hope in his eyes"—Kadek paused for effect as a smile crept across his face—"before I destroy him."

"Ingenious, m'lord."

"Leave me, Munson."

Munson whipped his tongue to lick the salty air and quietly slinked away.

The orangutan behind the bushes lifted his binoculars back up to his eyes, steadying his gaze upon the younger ape, who long ago watched their mother die and did nothing.

Yes, Arief. Soon you will greet me with a kiss. And then I will end everything you have built while you beg me for the mercy our mother never received.

ACKNOWLEDGMENTS

This sequel was mapped out and written entirely during the COVID-19 pandemic. It was a great time to be stuck at home with a book to write, but of course the pandemic was incredibly agonizing for everyone around the globe. I would like to use this opportunity to acknowledge the courageous sacrifices made by the world's health care workers and other frontline responders—and their families. And I want to spotlight the scientific and medical communities who identified and defined the threats, and who so rapidly developed vaccines and other strategies to tackle the global challenge we have faced.

I would like to thank everyone who helped nudge this project along during a difficult year, especially my family. Everest and Ariel, thanks for laughing in all the right places. Your encouragement strengthened me. Clare, you are of course my muse. You are the foundation for everything I succeed at in life.

And once again, to our own motley E-Team of adventurers and dreamers: Philippe Cousteau and his wife, Ashlan, and HarperCollins executive editor David Linker and his dedicated team. It has been the highlight of my writing career to partner with you all and to help make a positive difference in the world through your exemplary modeling of conservation optimism and action. And I'll finish with another shout-out to illustrator James Madsen. I'm so thrilled with the way you continue to bring the Endangereds to life.

—Austin Aslan

First I would like to thank my coauthor, Austin Aslan. His dedication, creativity, and passion for the Endangereds made this series come alive. I would like to thank my wife, Ashlan, for always believing in this project and for being such a patient listener to the countless versions, ideas, and rewrites that I subjected her to. To my little one, Vivienne, and my future little one, who will have just joined us by the time this book is published, you are my inspiration and have renewed my commitment to making this world a better place.

To our team at HarperCollins, thank you for your dedication to making these important stories a success, especially our executive editor, David Linker, who has been a tireless advocate for this project and an invaluable part of our small creative team. Finally, to James Madsen, who has brought these characters to life in such a caring and beautiful way, thank you.

—Philippe Cousteau

ABOUT THE ANIMALS

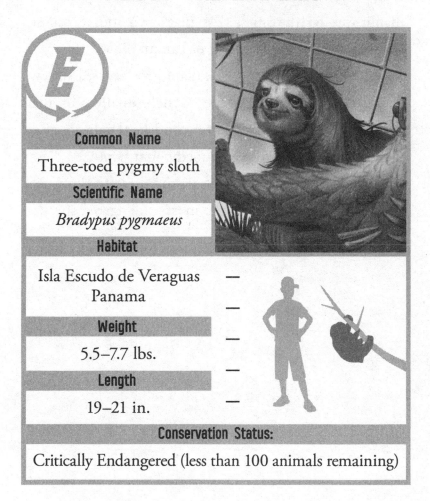

Common Name

Three-toed pygmy sloth

Scientific Name

Bradypus pygmaeus

Habitat

Isla Escudo de Veraguas
Panama

Weight

5.5–7.7 lbs.

Length

19–21 in.

Conservation Status:

Critically Endangered (less than 100 animals remaining)

LEARN MORE:

The three-toed pygmy sloth is the smallest sloth species
on Earth and also the most endangered, with fewer than

50 members of the species exclusively inhabiting the red mangroves on the small (less than two square miles) island of Escudo off the coast of Panama.

These sloths eat mainly mangrove leaves, which puts them under threat due to deforestation of the mangroves. In addition, hunting and feral cats are also putting pressure on the three-toed pygmy sloth.

Due to their small population, the three-toed pygmy sloth is considered one of the most endangered species on the planet.

HONU

Common Name

Pacific green sea turtle

Scientific Name

Chelonia mydas agassizii

Habitat

Pacific Ocean from Alaska to Chile

Weight

150–419 lbs.

Height

2.5–5 ft.

Conservation Status:

Endangered

LEARN MORE:

Sea turtles spend nearly their entire lives at sea. Only females and babies spend any time on land—females to lay eggs and babies to hatch. And as soon as those babies hatch, they make a mad dash to the sea.

Green sea turtles, unlike other sea turtles, are herbivores. Eating lots of algae and seagrass makes the fat under their shells green, hence their name. They live all over the world and are the largest of all the hard-shell sea turtles.

Some scientists consider the Pacific green sea turtle to be a unique species; some consider it to be a subspecies.

The biggest threats to sea turtles are marine debris like plastic that they may mistake for food and choke on, fishing lines that can wrap them up and prevent them from surfacing for air, getting caught in fishing nets, and their eggs being harvested for food (often illegally).

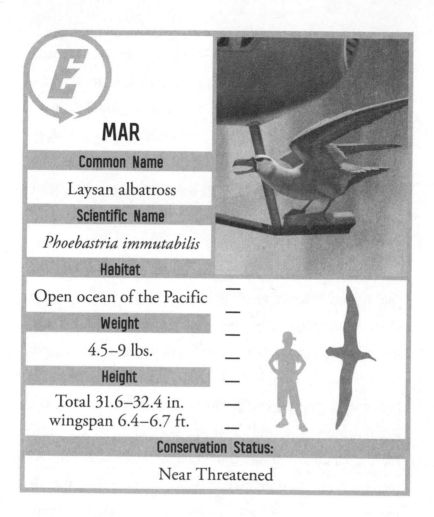

MAR

Common Name

Laysan albatross

Scientific Name

Phoebastria immutabilis

Habitat

Open ocean of the Pacific

Weight

4.5–9 lbs.

Height

Total 31.6–32.4 in.
wingspan 6.4–6.7 ft.

Conservation Status:

Near Threatened

LEARN MORE:

Albatrosses are equipped with a locking system within the joints of their wings that keeps their wings in the open position without requiring the birds to expend any additional energy. Given the enormous span of their wings along with this unique locking system, albatrosses are known as exceptional gliders. They can remain airborne for months at a time, covering a distance of more than 9,300 miles in a single trip! That's roughly equivalent to flying from New York City to Sydney, Australia, nonstop.

Albatrosses spend nearly their entire lives over the sea, feeding primarily on fish and squid, but they can also scavenge for food or dine on crustaceans, zooplankton, and other small animals.

Because they can live for more than sixty years, they're highly selective when choosing a mate. Courtship involves preening each other, dancing, and singing. Every few years they return to the same colony where they were born to mate, a habit called natal nesting. The female lays one egg, then the partners take turns tending the egg/chick and hunting for food. The proud parents care for the chick for about four to nine months before it's ready to set out on its own. The young bird then spends the first few years of its life at sea, without touching land.

There are twenty-two different species of albatross. The Laysan albatross mostly lives in the Hawaiian Islands and is medium in size compared to other albatross species.

The main threats to albatrosses are entanglement in fishing nets, getting caught on long line fishing hooks, mistaking plastic debris as food, and pollution.

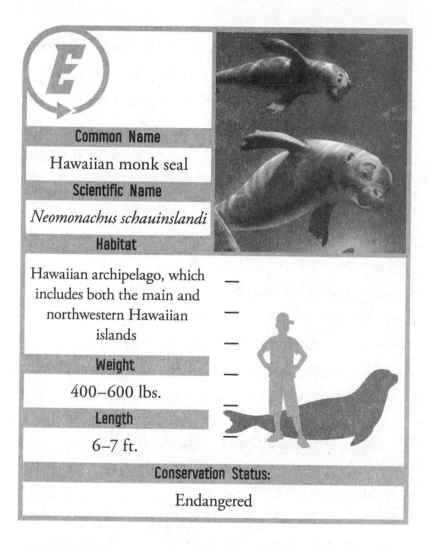

Common Name	
Hawaiian monk seal	
Scientific Name	
Neomonachus schauinslandi	
Habitat	
Hawaiian archipelago, which includes both the main and northwestern Hawaiian islands	
Weight	
400–600 lbs.	
Length	
6–7 ft.	
Conservation Status:	
Endangered	

LEARN MORE:

The Hawaiian monk seal, so named because they only live around the Hawaiian Islands, is one of the most endangered seal species in the world. Adults are dark gray or brown on their back and light gray on their stomachs. Hawaiian monk seals are "generalist" feeders, which means they eat a wide variety of foods depending on what's available. They eat many types of common fish, squids, octopuses, eels, and crustaceans like crabs and lobster. They prefer hunting for their food under rocks along the bottom of the sea floor.

Monk seal populations are currently about a third of their historic numbers, but their population is slowly increasing. The main threats to the monk seal's survival include plastic debris, overfishing (which limits availability of food), entanglement in fishing gear, pollution, illegal hunting (they are a fully protected species in Hawaii), and habitat loss.

MORE ABOUT THE ANIMALS

ABOUT ORANGUTANS:

Famous for their distinctive red or orange fur, orangutans are the largest arboreal (tree-dwelling) mammals in the world. These great apes have long, powerful arms and feet and hands that can grasp branches, allowing them to largely spend their mostly solitary lives in trees.

The word orangutan means "man of the forest" in the native Malay language, and, like humans, they are omnivores, meaning they eat both plants and animals. Their diet consists of wild fruits like lychees, mangosteens, and figs, but also ants and termites.

Orangutans are found on both the islands of Borneo and Sumatra and each population differs slightly in appearance and behavior. For example, Sumatran orangutans are reported to have closer social bonds than their Bornean cousins, but both species have experienced sharp population declines. A century ago, there were probably more than 230,000 orangutans in total. Today, Bornean orangutans number around 100,000 and are considered endangered, while Sumatran orangutans number about 7,500 and are considered critically endangered. Orangutans are threatened by deforestation and illegal capture for the wildlife trade.

A third species of orangutan was revealed through genetic analysis in 2017. With no more than 800 individuals in existence, the Tapanuli (an isolated region in southern Sumatra) orangutan is the most endangered of all great apes.

ABOUT POLAR BEARS:

As top carnivores, polar bears are critical to the health of the Arctic ecosystem. They are a formidable predator and the largest bear in the world. They are also the only species of bear considered a marine mammal, because they spend most of their lives on sea ice in the Arctic Ocean. While polar bears may be famous for their white coat of hollow hairs (the air in their fur helps them stay warm) their skin is actually black, which helps them absorb heat from the sun.

Polar bears mostly eat seals and other marine mammals.

Because of shrinking sea ice due to climate change, polar bears are an endangered species and continue to suffer the effects of humanity's dependance on fossil fuels.

ABOUT NARWHALS:

The narwhal, often called the "unicorn of the sea" because of the long, spiraled tusk that juts out of its head, is a marine mammal that lives in the Arctic waters of Canada, Russia, Norway, and Greenland. They feed on cod, shrimp, and squid. The tusk is actually an enlarged tooth, and scientists believe it is used to sense the environment around the narwhal. Males may also use it to exert dominance over other males.

Like polar bears, narwhals are primarily threatened by climate change and melting sea ice, which is transforming the entire ecosystem.

ABOUT BLACK-BELLIED PANGOLINS:

The black-bellied pangolin, otherwise known as the long-tailed pangolin (because its tail can be twice as long as its body), is one of eight pangolin species found in Africa and Asia.

Even though pangolins may look like reptiles because they are covered in scales, they are mammals. They use the scales for protection, rolling into a ball to defend themselves from predators.

Pangolins are solitary and usually nocturnal, or active at night, and feed mostly on ants and termites.

Tragically, pangolins are one of the most trafficked animals in the world. Usually hunted for their meat and scales, pangolins are starting to disappear because of the illegal wildlife trade. While they are mostly sold into illegal markets in Africa and Asia, there is growing demand for pangolin leather in the United States for products like boots and belts.

HOW YOU CAN BE A PART OF THE ADVENTURE AND HELP NATURE WITH EARTHECHO INTERNATIONAL:

Dear Reader,

I hope that you've enjoyed *The Endangereds: Melting Point*. As the second book in this series, I hope that it serves as a reminder to you that anyone can change the world—especially you.

Sixteen years ago, I founded an organization called EarthEcho International because I believed in the power that youth have to be champions for the natural world. Since then, I have seen countless young people do extraordinary things all over the planet—young people like you who care about animals and the environment and are passionate about taking action in their communities and around the world to protect and restore what we call our ocean planet.

At EarthEcho we are building a global youth move-ment for the environment and have lots of different programs that are designed to help you learn and take action. Our youth leaders have passed laws, raised crit-ical funds, started movements to protect land, founded successful businesses that help people and the planet, and so much more.

I know it seems like there is a lot of bad news about the environment these days, but I also know that there is tremendous hope. I have been all over the world and it is the optimism and determination that I see on the faces of young people just like you that reminds me of how much good there is in the world. By joining us, you will become part of a community of young people who recognize that when we come together, just like Nuk, Arief, Wan, and Murdock, there is nothing that we can-not achieve, no problem we cannot overcome, and no one who can stop us from building a better world.

—Philippe Cousteau